PURCHASED AT PUBLIC SALE
SURPLUS MATERIALS FROM THE SLCLS

HARLEM GLORY

Omar thundered
from the corner of Seventh Avenue:
"We colored folks need glorious bodies
and not glorious souls.
This is the age of the New Deal
and a new society is forming.
Are we going to keep on hoping and waiting
like Uncle Tom in the white folks' backyard
or get up and get in on the New Deal
to build up our colored communities
on the other side of the tracks?
That is the question I am asking in Harlem.
Where are the colored leaders leading
the colored people?
That is the question you people must ask.
You got to bellow it loud and long
until the leaders they get scared.
Worry them to death
until they give you the answer."

CLAUDE McKAY

D0838670

CHARLES H. KERR RADICAL FICTION

Claude McKay

Claude McKay

HARLEM GLORY

*A Fragment of
Aframerican Life*

Preface by Carl Cowl

CHICAGO
Charles H. Kerr Publishing Company
1990

BOOKS BY CLAUDE McKAY

Constab Ballads (1912)
Songs of Jamaica (1912)
Spring in New Hampshire (1920)
Harlem Shadows (1922)
Home to Harlem (1928; reprinted 1965, 1973)
Banjo (1929; reprinted 1970)
Gingertown (1932; reprinted 1972)
Banana Bottom (1933; reprinted 1961, 1971, 1974)
A Long Way From Home (1937; reprinted 1970, 1985)
Harlem: Negro Metropolis (1940; reprinted 1968)

Published Posthumously

Selected Poems of Claude McKay (1953; reprinted 1968)
Dialect Poetry of Claude McKay (1972)
The Passion of Claude McKay:
Selected Poetry and Prose (1973)
My Green Hills of Jamaica (1979)
The Negro in America (1979)
Harlem Glory (1990)

ISBN 0-88286-162-x *cloth*
0-88286-163-8 *paper*

On the Cover:
"Jam Session," by Tristan Meinecke (1942)

First edition

© Copyright 1990
Charles H. Kerr Publishing Company

 594

Send for our complete catalog.
Charles H. Kerr Publishing Company
Established 1886
P. O. Box 914
Chicago, Illinois 60626

PREFACE

1990 marks the hundredth anniversary of the birth of Claude McKay, born September 15th, 1890 in Sunny Ville, Clarendon Parish, Jamaica. Over two generations have passed since he died in Chicago in 1948. An almost tangible reawakening of interest in the man and his message seems to have emerged in recent times.

Long before he wrote his last book, *Harlem Glory*—published here for the first time—McKay had earned recognition for his unique and distinctive Jamaican dialect poetry, his rebel pioneering in the Harlem literary upsurge of the 1920s, and his influence on the rise of the Negritude movement of Africa and Europe.

Ironically, most of his best fiction—*Home to Harlem* (1928), *Banjo* (1929), *Gingertown* (1932), *Banana Bottom* (1933), and the still-unpublished *Romance in Marseilles*—was written as an expatriate in France and Morocco. Largely because of the success of *Home to Harlem* he returned to the United States in 1934 a world-famous author, only to be engulfed in the misery of the Great Depression and the ruthlessness of a society intolerant of criticism. Soon reduced to poverty, McKay also suffered from a slowly progressive illness from which he never recovered.

Prior to his career as a novelist, McKay had published several volumes of poetry and edited Max Eastman's *Liberator* magazine—the successor to the *Masses* after it was suppressed by the government for its militant opposition to World War I. His experiences in the labor movement are reflected in his novels, especially in *Home to Harlem* and *Harlem Glory*. In this early period he also wrote his first work of non-fiction, *The Negro in America*. This short study was commissioned by the Communist International after McKay's full-length presentation of the subject to the Fourth Congress in December, 1922, and published in Moscow in 1923 in Russian translation. The original English manuscript has never been found.

He wrote his autobiography, *A Long Way from Home* (published in 1937), followed by *Harlem: Negro Metropolis* (1940), a collection of essays dealing with the cultural and political life of the depressed black urban community of the Thirties: the phenomenon of Father Divine, whom tens of thousands worshipped as God; the grass-roots labor movement led by Sufi Abdul Hamid and Ira Kemp; Marcus Garvey's Black Star Back-to-Africa movement; the "occultists"; the numbers racket; the amusement business; the black businessmen and politicians. There was also a chapter on West Indian and Hispanic social relations. Engagingly written, perceptive, thoughtful and novel, it was also argumentative, and frankly critical of the racism of white radical parties, including the Communist and Socialist parties. The book had a poor reception.

Interestingly enough, while writing *Harlem: Negro Metropolis*, McKay was also writing a work of fiction covering similar ground. These scenes of the daily life he had found in Depression Harlem after his return from overseas evolved into his last novel, *Harlem Glory*. By disguising real-life characters and groups behind pseudonyms, Claude evidently hoped that this quasi-autobiographical account would prove more acceptable to readers than a straight, unvarnished, non-fiction treatment offered in *Harlem: Negro Metropolis*. Thus Buster South, the hero of *Harlem Glory*, returns to Harlem in the Thirties, as did McKay, after his stay abroad. He becomes involved in movements agitating the community. In this book Father Divine becomes "Glory Savior," and Sufi Abdul Hamid (whose very effective boycott during the early 1930s forced Harlem merchants to hire black employees) emerges as "Omar." Omar's triumphant organization is here called "Yeomen of Labor."

McKay's hostility to the Communist Party found in *Harlem: Negro Metropolis* also appears in the novel. None of the characters, in fact, are Communists. Nonetheless, several characters in the book, and by no means the least attractive among them, are outspoken radicals. Indeed, throughout *Harlem Glory*—and especially in the chapters on the Yeomen of Labor and Buster's experiences at a New Deal work-camp—it is clear that McKay continued to favor the radical transformation of society, but definitely not as envisioned by the Communist Party. Here and there one can discern his experiences as a member of the Industrial Workers of the World (IWW) in 1919. In *The Negro in America* he had emphasized that the IWW, alone among American labor organizations, had accepted blacks as equals. In the same book McKay had argued that the Communist Party had not matched the IWW's record in this regard. In *Home to Harlem* one of the central characters, Jake Brown, tells a Wobbly organizer that, while longshoring in Philadelphia, he had been "a good union man." Some believe that McKay had belonged at one time to the IWW's Marine Transport Workers Industrial Union 510, whose Philadelphia leader, Ben Fletcher, was the best known of the IWW's black organizers. Writing *Harlem Glory* in the late 1940s, when the IWW had long since ceased to be a major factor in the labor movement, McKay never ceased regarding black-white workingclass solidarity as the prerequisite for solving the contradictions of capitalist society. The sections of the novel that have to do with labor organization have a Wobbly flavor. In colorful language, Omar, the black labor organizer, repudiates the slogan of "Defend the Soviet Union!" promulgated by the Communist Party as well as by the Trotskyists and other leftists, and favors instead the slogan, "Defend Black America!"

In his biography of McKay, Wayne Cooper describes *Harlem Glory* as "apparently unfinished." It is true that the abrupt ending leaves some of the conflicts, stories and tensions unresolved. It should be remembered, however, that McKay's novelistic approach differed from that of most other writers of fiction. The author of *Banjo*—which is significantly subtitled "A Story Without a Plot"—simply did not share the concerns of those who believe that every loose narrative thread must be neatly tied up in the end. In this sense, McKay was a truer realist than many writers who had borne this label, for life itself he considered "A Story Without a Plot." In any case, although we have no way of knowing how he might have concluded this tale, *Harlem Glory* stands as a powerful narrative, a vivid portrayal of social ferment, and among the finest of McKay's writings.

The politically forbidding climate of the 1940s, and the scary McCarthy period of the Fifties, caused publishers to shy away from this novel, with its searing criticisms.

It was a great source of regret to me personally, that, after he made me his literary agent in 1943, he did not live to see this book in print.

On this occasion, therefore, in the last decade of the century, when political winds are shifting, Hope McKay Virtue—Claude's daughter—and I salute the Charles H. Kerr Company for seizing this moment to honor Claude McKay on the hundredth anniversary of his birth.

Carl Cowl

New York,
May 1, 1990

Table of Contents

1
BUSTER ABROAD

I t was ending of summer. The mighty horde of short-term vacationists were leaving Europe to return home for Labor Day. Many long-term residents were fleeing from the increasing cost of existence in France for an easier life in Spain or elsewhere. But Buster South remained, celebrating success in Paris. Having no income or a job, Buster was nevertheless living elegantly without responsibility or being unnecessarily beholden.

Back in Harlem there were many inelegant comments about Buster's residing abroad. The sharpest originated among close acquaintances, mostly male, none of whom would have hesitated in doing precisely what Buster had done.

Buster had quit the Harlem scene, adroitly disappearing with the receding wave of the vast intricate undercover industry of numerology. Like hundreds of others in Harlem, Buster had once existed nicely from that clandestine industry. But unlike many who were in the business as bankers, controllers, collectors, Buster actually was never connected with it.

He had enjoyed his sinecure through his friendship with Millinda Rose, een, and the most extravagantly dashing creature of the numbers Harlem. Coming up out of the deep South with nothing but his 's lamp in his hand, all through the narrow devious ways of black belts, Buster had so dexterously manipulated his magic that it had carried him finally straight into the exclusive circle of Harlem's fast set. He was spotted and appreciated by Millinda Rose and favored with her confidence and intimacy. Buster often accompanied Millinda to fashionable functions and became generally known as her escort.

Millinda was the consort of Ned Rose, the late Policy King. Ned Rose was the first Harlem banker to lift the numbers game to an apparently respectable level, when instead of carrying on the business in a barber shop or a shoe-shine kiosk, he made over an entire first-floor apartment into a numbers bank and employed regular clerks. He grew wealthy. Besides the numbers business he also was the owner of a first-class tonsorial parlor. He met Millinda when she began working there as a manicurist.

Millinda had come to Harlem from Virginia. Although quite young, she had been a village schoolteacher back home. She could not teach anything in New York, of course, for her rudimentary education was far below the required standard. She went to work as a domestic and during spare time attended a beauty school. When she had completed her course, she quit domestic service.

That afternoon when Ned was attracted by Millinda he had visited his tonsorial parlor for a shave only. He was wearing a black band on his arm, for his wife had recently died. Although he was becoming extremely wealthy, as the numbers business expanded and hundreds of Harlemites preferred to gamble with his bank because of its reputation of being reliable and long-established, Ned Rose was not given to extravagant living. But when he saw Millinda, he thought he would try a manicure, instead of paring his fingernails himself as he always did.

So Ned placed his heavy ebony hand in Millinda's little amber hand and realized a thrill. Stroking his fingers, she touched his feeling. From then he started courting Millinda. He invited her out to dinner. He called for her in his car to take her home after she had finished working. Millinda did not remain very long in the tonsorial parlor. Ned installed her in his office, making her his assistant.

The barbers discussed Millinda's quick promotion to a better job. A young barber (who had unsuccessfully tried to win her attention) commented to an older.

Young barber: A woman what's a good looker more'n or'nary is always a big manipulator. I works mah hands tiahed day and night and can't evah make a raise.

Second young barber (sucking his teeth with a contemptuo[us] Working with you' hands, fellah. Don't you realize yet that work[ ] you' hands kain't get a man or a woman any place? It's working y[our head].

First young barber: You ain't telling me nothing. It was Millinda's hands got her where she is, she working with her hands on somebody's hands was what got her a raise.

Old barber: Young man, you-all should understand that a woman nacherally possesses more ways than a man of making a raise. What good you-all stahting an argument about hands and heads? It's neither one nor

the other only. It's hands and heads and feets working together in this great game of life since Adam and Eve. When I was your age a real man was never jealous of a woman's ways, but in these heah days—
Young barber: It ain't that I feel jealous. Ah'm jest turning Millinda over in mah mind.
Old barber: Don't son, bettah forget her and attach your ambition to a possibility.

Numbers King Ned Rose made Millinda his Numbers Queen. They were married in fine style. Harlem enjoyed another big West Indian wedding. Ned Rose was a West Indian and the West Indians adore sumptuous ceremonies. He and Millinda were married in the colored Episcopal church, with two preachers assisting in the ritual and six sugar-brown maids attending Millinda. All of them wore the same frocks, which Millinda had chosen and for which Ned paid. A cavalcade of cars paraded the company along Seventh Avenue up to Sugar Hill. There was a big feast in Ned's apartment. Dominating the table was the huge wedding cake, specially made by the accomplished West Indian cake-makers of Harlem. There were gallons of rum-runners' booze and happy feet shuffled to the banging of a Harlem orchestra.

2
NUMBERS MAGIC

In those days white New York was unaware that black Harlem also had a way of gambling on the Stock Exchange. It was first known as the West Indian game. They were West Indians who originally worked out the device of taking figures from the Stock Exchange Sales to establish a daily lottery. It was printed on cards of the visiting variety, thus:

STOCKS AND BONDS
New York Stock Exchange Sales

Day Sales *$2,560,000*
Bond Sales *10,110,000*
Curb Sales *75,000*

WINNING NUMBER
617
TIME TO PLAY: Weekdays until 2 p.m.
Saturday until noon

— —

See Winning Number in the 7th Star Newspaper

The game attracted the poorest of the colored masses, for the placing of one cent was as readily accepted as five or ten or twenty-five cents. Generally a dollar was the maximum amount played. Five cents played on a lucky number won thirty dollars for the player. Of this amount three dollars was retained by the agent, called a collector.

The winning number appeared in the latest editions of the evening papers. All the players knew the device and picked it out of the financial figures. Winners were paid late in the evening or the following morning. Hardly a day passed without a few persons winning or, as they say, "hitting the number."

The principals in the game were "bankers," "controllers," "runners" and "collectors." The collector possessed the slips on which the individual bets (numbers with amounts) were recorded. He was entitled to twenty per cent of all monies collected, besides ten per cent commission on the winning number. The runner visited districts outside of the Harlem area to pick up money from the collectors. His work was very important. For it was possible for him to operate in collusion with a collector to cheat the banker. For example, he could arrange with a collector to put the winning number on a slip *after* it had appeared in the evening papers and the playing had "legally" stopped, and then stage an automobile accident to delay him. Faced with the proof of an accident the banker was obliged to pay the winner. For this reason a runner was always a trusted relative or confidante of the banker. He was paid an adequate weekly salary by the banker. The controller was go-between for collector and banker. He received the slips from collectors, which he placed in envelopes, one envelope for each collector. These he turned in with monies collected to the banker. Many collectors did business with controllers only, without knowing who was the banker. An able and popular controller had dozens of collectors working for him. He might handle from $250 to over $1000 every playing day. The banker paid him ten per cent of all collections under his control. In addition he received a weekly bonus of three per cent on the gross of all monies that he turned in to the bank.

The banker was the mystery man. The majority of players and collectors often knew that an individual was their responsible banker, without having a speaking acquaintanceship with him. Especially if he were a successful banker. His office was usually located in a large room of an apartment or a private house. It was equipped with large tables for assorting the slips, many adding machines for recording the numbers and a typewriter or two.

The clerks were carefully chosen and constantly watched. Sometimes a new clerk was planted in an office to keep tab on others. They were not supposed to carry pencils into the office. For it was possible for them to have an arrangement with a collector or controller by which they could write the winning number on his slip while assorting. And the money thus won would be divided between the principals. But some clerks even outwitted bankers by concealing pencil points beneath their fingernails. Each clerk received a salary of about twenty-five dollars a week.

As the numbers game grew to large proportions in Harlem, the circulation of certain evening newspapers was increased there. When the circulation department of one newspaper investigated and discovered the cause of its increased circulation, it placarded the newsstands in Harlem with the advertisement: FIRST OUT WITH THE WINNING NUMBER.

Naturally this helped increase the vogue of numbers in Harlem. The ignorant masses were excited by the idea of their big Negroes understanding the magic of the Stock Exchange and working out a plan in which all Harlem could participate. And all of Harlem played with numbers: the humble laundrywoman and the disreputable pool player as well as the respectable schoolteacher.

The chances of winning were increased by the combination plan. This was six ways of playing a given number. Thus the number 915 could be resolved into six components like this:

915
519
159
195
591
951

If the sum of sixty cents was placed on this number, ten cents would be allotted to each component. And if it were a lucky number, the winner got sixty dollars.

As the game gripped the imagination of the Harlem masses, the business of numbers magic flourished. Negroes became canny about numbers. Any number seen, or which came to one's mind under unusual circumstances, would be played. Persons considered good at guessing winning numbers were said to possess occult powers. Some of them started a business of selling hot numbers. Significant dreams were translated into numbers. An enterprising Negro published the first Dream Book of numbers. It became Harlem's best-seller, going into many editions within a few months. Other dream books were published. The show windows of drugstores and candy stores rivaled each other with striking advertisements of Dream Books of numbers such as : *Lucky Star, Combination, Red Witch, Prince Ali, Gypsy Witch, Afro-Indian, Afrabian, Egyptian, Golden Success, Moses Magical, Moe-and-Joe* and *Policy Pete.*

Some of the authors were white. For the success of the first Negro book immediately brought white competitors into the Harlem field. Even as the success of the numbers game attracted white "bankers" to Harlem, white residents avidly started playing the thing they had formerly contemptuously referred to as "the nigger pool."

As dreams developed more meaning and business in Harlem, conjury and voodooism assumed a larger significance and some practitioners blossomed as spiritualists.

A vast new field of exploitation was opened up in Harlem, through the ramifications of the numbers game. That clandestine industry reached its peak in the decade following the world war. Most of the stations where the numbers were deposited were also depots of bootleg liquor. Harlem was the paradise of bootleggers, and many of them had developed an interest in the numbers game when they learned of the fabulous profits of the big black operators. Prohibition had made the defiance of the laws general and racketeering respectable. Some of the most law-abiding citizens patronized bootleggers.

The heavy rumble of underhand business swelled the natural noise of Harlem. There was an abundance of easy, parasitic jobs. The numbers bankers exhibited the most expensive cars and equipped the most expensive apartments and acquired country houses in Connecticut and Long Island. Locally they were known as numbers millionaires.

3
HOSTESS OF HARLEM

Buster's early career had paralleled Millinda's. Both had traveled from out of the deep South in quest of a larger life in the North. Their destiny had brought them together in Harlem. But Millinda had covered a more easily romantic road. Her happy marriage had projected her into a position luxurious beyond her wildest imagination.

Harlem had no real knowledge of the extent of the wealth which Ned Rose had acquired from the operation of the numbers game. With the spreading of the game far and wide, many new bankers had sprung up who were flashy livers. They spun around Harlem in splendid cars, set the pace in stylish clothes, and were prominent at smart social functions.

But Ned Rose had preferred to live quietly. His first wife was a West Indian, who was unknown in Harlem society. He had identified himself with the less spectacular way of life. He gave money to the Colored Orphanage, the Negro Aid Association, and the Negro churches. He also played a leading role in his fraternal lodge. When the lodge was in financial difficulties, Ned undertook its reorganization and finally pulled it up on its feet again.

He established, through the lodge, scholarships for the higher education of impoverished students. Often sneered at as a racketeer by more respectable Harlemites, he nevertheless was extremely charitable. He gave money even to a charitable white institution, which gave aid to poor white intellectuals. Some of his critics called his gifts "atonement money."

However, while Ned lived like a dignified, middle-aged businessman, Millinda was attracted to the smart, pace-making set. She adored dancing and parties. Moving from Harlem-under-the-hill to Sugar Hill, she started entertaining. And as soon as the fast set became aware of Millinda and her command of big money, she was flattered with many invitations. Millinda responded with her own invitations and soon had the satisfaction of having at her house the leading stars of the amusement world and members of the professional elite of Harlem. It was at this time that Buster South came into her life. Buster was the black Beau Brummell of the fast set. He was a splendid dancer and much desired as a partner by the fashionable dames. Millinda became specially interested in him. Perhaps it was because, like herself, he did not legitimately belong to the smart, professional, and educated group of colored folk. Only by the magic of his Aladdin's lamp had he horned his way there, even as she had with her feminine charm and power. Ned Rose gave Millinda his passive support. He was proud of her excelling as Harlem's hostess: it was a new and novel world for him. But he appreciated the modern trends of life. And though Millinda liked to make large social gestures, she was a wise and careful housekeeper.

Most interesting were some white friends of the smart colored set who visited their house. For it was at that time that Harlem was hectic with frequent and huge winnings in the numbers game, and tall tales of its kings and queens, incredible like oriental fantasies, were being circulated, that the quarter attracted a certain coterie of whites. These whites were a different set from the creatures of the underworld who have always patronized colored amusement places. They were members of the ultra- sophisticated literati and the bohemian fringe of New York's intelligentsia. Besides an amazingly wide-open wet area of speakeasies and cabarets, they found that there existed in Harlem an exclusive, extraordinarily highly-developed dark bohemia and an aspiring little literati. They also discovered Millinda and Buster.

Mainly it was through Millinda that the white reading world became aware of the numbers game. There were journalists among the white visitors. Excited and delighted by her sumptuously furnished home and her luxurious way of living, they were astounded when they learned that her husband had acquired his wealth through the manipulation of the Harlem lottery. And soon titillating items about the Harlem game began appearing in the national newspapers.

The colored newspapers reproduced such items, and the eyes of the colored journalists were opened to a field that they were daily trampling underfoot and yet never saw. All of colored America looked to the goldmine of Harlem as the numbers game was touted as a million dollar business.

Hot numbers were peddled on the street corner to the credulous masses by the diviners and interpreters of numbers. Not so crudely and visibly operating were the mysterious tipsters. A couple of shrewd Harlemites had established a connection by which they could obtain knowledge of the Stock Exchange figures in advance of their publication. Through a special clique of players they often played the lucky number, and their winnings were heavy. The clique was organized not to break the numbers bankers, but to obtain a maximum of their heavy profits. The bankers were convinced that there was a leak, but could not trace the tipsters.

There was one week, however, when even the clique was tricked, and the real lucky number was tipped off to the Harlem public. Whisperings ran like rats down the ways of Harlem: "Play number 772." That number was heavily played and it was the winning one. Thousands of dollars had to be paid out. The banks cracked. When the players discovered that the bankers were bankrupt, some bloody battles were staged in Harlem. Enraged, they patrolled the streets, hunting collectors and controllers, savagely beating and even knifing them. One big banker was shot dead in a hallway. Some went into hiding; others took a sea change over to Cuba, Jamaica and Trinidad.

About six big bankers on that wild day had closed their banks, having been warned not to send out their collectors to take numbers. Among them was Ned Rose. With the other banks ruined, the big six reorganized and consolidated the numbers business in their hands.

The publicity given the wild riot of numbers attracted the manipulators of the white underworld business to the game. These buccaneers were already powerful in Harlem as the vast depot of bootleg liquor. They knew of the existence of the numbers game but had contemptuously dismissed it as the "nigger pool," which was unworthy of their attention. But now they realized that thousands of dollars were being made out of those "nigger nickels."

The underworld whites were initiated into the ways of operating the numbers game by some of the ruined colored bankers, who acted in a spirit of revenge and also with the hope of starting in again with white protectors. The white operators established a chain of cigar stores as a front for operating the game. They broadened its scope by establishing banks in other cities, exciting the white population to play. And soon Harlem's numbers game was being played ardently by white and colored in all the great American cities.

Also trouble began shooting between the white bankers and the colored bankers. The white syndicate was determined to bring the entire field of the numbers game under its control. It ordered the colored number kings to join the syndicate; otherwise, they would be driven out of the field. A few of the blacks capitulated, but the big six held out. The whites threatened them and then went into action. One big black banker was kidnapped and held for thousands of dollars ransom. The ransom was paid, but it broke his bank. Another, hounded and pursued, finally had the top of his expensive car blown off by machine-gun. Miraculously he escaped injury. He was warned that on the next occasion it would be sure death. He joined the syndicate. One who would not heed the warnings of the syndicate, not taking them seriously, was hurled down a shaftway.

But Ned Rose refused to join the syndicate. He and Millinda put their heads together and it was decided that Ned should take a sea change and visit the West Indies. After Ned's departure, Millinda gave up entertaining to concentrate upon holding the intricate threads of the numbers business together and beating the white syndicate. She used her woman's wits. Headstrong Ned was bitter against the white competitors, denouncing them for entering the circumscribed field of black racketeering and had vowed that he would never join them in exploiting his people in that game.

But Millinda thought differently. She shared Ned's resentment. She also hated "white trash." But the white people she had known in the South were a little different in many ways from those that Ned had known in the West Indies, and that made a difference in determining their respective attitudes, even though they were emotionally united in their feeling of hostility. Millinda's background was dominated by individuals of the colored group who were protected by influential white people, and it did not matter that the white people referred to them as "good niggers" and the resentful colored people as "white folks' niggers." That protection was a real concrete thing.

There were two groups of the white underworld disputing the Harlem field: one was Italian, the other Jewish. Millinda's bootlegger was an Italian. He introduced her to the Italian group. She negotiated with them and sold out some of her business, with the understanding that she was to obtain protection for herself. When she had the transaction completed and everything settled, she brought Ned back from the West Indies.

By that time municipal and federal investigators were aroused and hot on the heels of Harlem; for the marvelous tales of its brazen bootleg and magical numbers manner of existence had penetrated to the sanctums of law and order. Accompanied by nationwide publicity, there began an official investigation of the numbers game. The police found it expedient at last to pick up scores of collectors with slips, acting as if they were not all along acquainted with all such persons and their business.

The collectors laughed and said that the police played the numbers regularly, like everybody else in Harlem. Nevertheless hundreds of collectors, controllers, and other numbers game officials were arrested and brought to trial, but most of them were eventually released.

The large bank accounts of the bankers were uncovered. But Ned Rose's was not. For when he was abroad, Millinda had drawn out their money from different banks and placed it in one bank, where no government investigators imagined a Negro would have an account. Meanwhile Ned was still hiding in Harlem. He and Millinda agreed to depart secretly for Europe and remain there until the noise about the numbers had died down. On the eve of sailing Ned visited the Submarine Speakeasy, whose owner was his friend. It was rather early and there were few customers besides the waiters. Ned stood at the bar talking to the proprietor. A man walked up to him and cried: "You can't get away with everything," and pumped bullets into his guts.

Millinda cremated Ned. And she resolved to take that vacation in Europe as they had planned. She had lost interest in the numbers business and sold out what was left of it.

4
BEATING THE RAP

Buster accompanied Millinda to Paris. Millinda was proud of her wits. She had not only outwitted some of the cunningest brains of the white underworld, but also the legal authority which was investigating the giant octopus of the business of gangsterism, one of whose white tentacles held firmly the little black bastard body of black racketeering. Millinda was especially happy that, unlike other policy operators, her name had not appeared in the newspapers, dragging along with it her nice colored and white acquaintances.

"How long are we going to stay?" asked Buster. "Just as long as we like staying," Millinda said, "at least until the big white noise over a little nigger racketeering is hushed up. Are you worried?" "Not me," said Buster, "not for mahself, so long as your affairs can stand it." "I'm finished with the numbers game, if that is what you mean," said Millinda. "It's easy making the money, but I'm tired of paying off for protection and for business. When Ned and I got married the numbers was quiet and good. We didn't have to pay off the police and the white gunmen…No, I'm through. When I start again, it will be an open, respectable business. I've got plenty of money to start in big."

Millinda did possess thousands of dollars. It appeared incredible that such large fortunes had been accumulated from the careless pennies and nickels of Harlem's army of domestic workers, earning five and ten dollars weekly, out of which they staked a penny, a nickel or a dime in the hope of winning 5 or 25 or 50 dollars extra to take a fling at Harlem life. What magic was held for the poor players in those thousands of little white policy slips tabulated with figures!

Millinda engaged rooms for herself and Buster in a large hotel on the Right Bank. Mainly she desired to forget the ways and the people of Harlem for a time and lose herself in strange surroundings, but she found quite a little of Harlem in Paris. There were many Aframerican musicians and actors, some out of work, also students and other colored Americans, like Millinda and Buster, enjoying a trip abroad.

The many unemployed colored persons made Millinda uncomfortable in her comfort. Indirectly and directly she received many requests for money. Although she was generally generous, she knew from experience that most people borrowed money with no intention of paying it back; it was just a respectable holdup. And she resented being held up. Life to her was one big numbers game, with everybody playing and only a few winning.

Inevitably Millinda and Buster met Lotta Sander, a bright-skinned young woman from Harlem, who had lived many years abroad. Lotta attached herself to the pair as a kind of indispensible chaperon. She introduced them into a mixed set of cosmopolites, including colored Americans, Africans, Europeans, and Asiatics. Lotta knew the bohemian ins and outs of Paris. She was not a professional entertainer nor a student, like most of the colored Americans abroad. Nor did she have an income. But she did have the great gift of charm and the asset of mixing easily with any group. A large part of her leisure time in Paris was devoted to visitors such as Millinda, who, however independent of character they may be, are glad to meet a friendly, helpful person in a strange capital.

Millinda and Buster were drawn into Lotta's circle of friends, meeting among others, Lotta's close friend, Austrian Baron Belchite, and also West African Prince Kuakoh Fanti, Miss Aschine Palma, a colored American with an income which enabled her to live on a middle-class level abroad, and Madame Audace, a lady with international connections who, reputedly, was related to influential persons in Europe and in America.

From European and American friends Madame Audace had heard of the hostess of Harlem, and she was eagerly interested in Millinda's gestures in Paris. In Harlem Millinda was notorious for her unguarded tongue: they said she was the one woman who would face another without anger and say exactly what she would behind her back. Because of that, Millinda was never mixed up in the petty squabbles of the black belt, although sometimes her lashing tongue precipitated a real fight. Millinda could shoot her words straight but without venom. Madame Audace thought Millinda ''a very healthy type.''

Millinda appreciated another colored woman putting her experiences of Paris at her disposal, but yet she was often irritated by Lotta. Lotta was over-possessed of the American passion of collecting souvenirs and would appropriate items which caught her fancy from public places as well as friends. Millinda missed little things such as a pin or earrings or a vial of perfume and even small banknotes left on the table. They were trifles, but perhaps more annoying to a woman when missing than more important things.

One day Millinda was especially irritated and explosive with rare expletives, when she discovered one missing from a pair of fancy French undies which she had purchased to take back to New York. The undies had appealed to her luxurious feelings even more than the fine French frocks: they were so different in style from the women's whimsies in New York.

Millinda had had a late breakfast and was still wearing her yellow pajamas and telling Buster, who had just entered the room, about the missing undies. "I don't like a woman who's a little snitcher," said Millinda. "She's like a tormenting pin worked loose in your clothes and hard to find."

The door opened and Lotta Sander entered. She was like a Barbary monkey, impish—appearing with a complexion like a fine ripe banana. "Hello," she said, airily waving her hand, "Hello you, Lotta, and listen first thing," said Millinda, "I don't like nobody around me with itchy fingers. Why did you snitch one of my undies? When I buy things for mahself I like to keep them for mahself."

Lotta's bright manner and color went flat. "Heck, what if I borrow one undies when you have a lot of them? I've been taking you all around and introducing you to everybody. What have I got for all the trouble?"

"If that's the way you feel about it, then may I ask who is paying for all the expensive food and liquor?"

"You were treating yourself. I was only a guide and interpreter," said Lotta with a dry laugh.

"I think I've been plenty nice to you, Lotta, since I came to Paris. But I see you're not satisfied. Now listen, I want to tell you this straight: no nigger running around and laying with a white person should ask another nigger for anything. Not if she is any good. Get me? Here you are giving your time and all to a white man—a baron you call him. But he doesn't look like any thing but a louse to me. He hasn't anything and you got nothing. What's the idea then? That damned title? Haven't you got some pride in your black hide to put a price on it, instead of messing around with a rotten title which is worth no more than a dead rat in a gutter? Since you're in the game why don't you play it right? Your old black mammy

23

had more sense than you. My husband made his money outta nigger nickels, and what I got from him I haven't gived to any white man. I entertain white folks alright, but they entertain me too. I nevah did lose mah haid ovah any white skin."

"Belchite is not cheap," said Lotta defiantly. "He's poor but—"

"Shut up or I'll make you!" cried Millinda. "You swipe my undies to go with that there damn thing. Baron, my foot! I don't want my stuff abused for such a purpose."

Lotta folded under Millinda's outburst, her bright yellow color fading away. "Stop, will you?" she said. "I feel rotten, more than you imagine. I've touched bottom."

"M'm," Millinda grunted. "Touch bottom. So you can't take it, eh?"

"Oh, it's not what you say why I said that. It's this messy life I'm living. You're right. I borrowed your undies and what good did that do? Last night Belchite took me to the Cong Vif. That place where all those lowdown Senegalese go. Remember, I took you there slumming. Belchite likes it, but I don't. The air is foul.

"A gang of Apaches and their women were there dancing the beguine with the Senegalese, but Belchite didn't want to dance. We just sat there liquoring up ourselves. The place was so close I felt like I was burning up under an African sun. So when we got home, it was nearly dawn, I was going to sponge off. And Belchite he begged me not to and said he wished I wouldn't always deodorize so much, because he was crazy about nigger odor."

"Good Lawd, be ye merciful," cried Buster, who all the time had kept quiet and out of the women's squabble. "This is a brand new one!" Millinda eagerly straightened up on the couch, her eyes big wild and strange like an excited cat.

"Oh, I was shocked out of my skin," said Lotta, "and I said I didn't think I smelled like a nigger. And he said that if I didn't he wouldn't like me because I'd be just like a colorless white female. So I asked if he really did mean that or was he joking. And he said indeed he did and that was why he liked the Congo Vif—it wasn't the jazzing, he preferred Viennese waltz—it was the odor which went to his head like champagne. Oh I tell you I feel dirty and lower than the lowest nigger in Harlem. I used to feel cleaner over there. Yet now I don't think I can ever go back. I'm sinking too low."

"No woman who says she's intelligent should let herself sink too low because of any man," said Millinda in a different tone—sympathetic, maternal—"even though this is a man's world and I mean a white man's world. You've got education—''

"Education!'' Lotta screamed. "Perhaps that's what's wrong. If I weren't educated I would fight like a bloody savage. Yes I would,'' and she rose striding across the room and shaking her fists.

The door opened abruptly and a tall gleaming black man entered with the air of a person who thought he could open all doors without knocking. His shoulders were wide, fine-angled, triangularly tapering down to narrow hips, making a splendid specimen of the finer species of West Africans.

It was the Prince Kuakok Fanti, a descendant of a deposed West African ruler. He had been sent to France as a youth, where he had received a liberal education. He spoke French, English, German, Arabic and his West African tongue. He existed on a small government pension, which he eked out by heavy borrowings from admirers of both sexes, which were never repaid. He was persona grata in the American Negro colony and introduced its smarter members to his European friends. American Negroes thought they were paying him a compliment when they said: "You don't look like an African any.''

Fanti and Lotta were friendly but not intimate. Lotta sometimes preferred his company to Baron Belchite on special occasions, when she desired to make an impression as an exotic type. For Fanti's blackness offset her yellowness and emphasized her Negroid features, which were not obvious to the casual eye.

"Fanti,'' said Millinda, "Lotta is carrying on like a sick cat, because her Baron Belchite admires African perfume.''

"African perfume? Why, they make fine perfume in Africa,'' said Fanti. "I don't understand?''

"Come on, Lotta,'' said Millinda, "tell Fanti about it or shall I?'' said Millinda, and promptly related the story herself.

Fanti shrugged, laughed. "I cannot find any offense there and I am African born and bred. In Africa the sense of smell is greater than of sight. We can smell animals before seeing them and we know the dangerous ones from the good ones. We can tell human beings by smell. What of it? We're a clean people. We bathe more than Europeans.''

"Guess that will satisfy you, Lotta,'' said Millinda. "The white and the black they both think the same thing.''

"That's sure tittering,'' said Buster.

"There's more than that to it,'' said Lotta, "but let's forget about it.''

"Sure thing,'' said Buster, "it's too much trouble, thinking black or thinking white. Niggers have nothing but feelings.''

"Any plans for today?'' asked Fanti.

"I'll blow the gang to Montmartre tonight," said Millinda. "I've been kinda mean and ornery like, but I'm going to be nice."

"I want to eat," said Buster.

"Me too," said Lotta.

"Well, you all go on and eat and find something to do afterwards," said Millinda. "I am going to the bank and will see you later."

"Hurry up and skip," said Fanti, standing and bowing gallantly. "The lady has *something more important* than us to think about now."

When they were gone, Millinda opened a drawer and extracted a large thick envelope. She checked up her letter of credit and found left 925 dollars. She counted a pad of American Express checks. She put the money in a large scarlet handbag, dressed, and went out.

Millinda's plump figure was well-preserved like a jar of candied ginger. She was aware that she attracted unusual attention as she pushed through the revolving doors of the great American bank in Paris. Involuntarily she glanced at the mirror attached to her bag and adjusted the black hat, with long sloping feather that sat upon her head like a soup ladle. It was supposed to represent the style of the Empress Eugenie.

She tripped up to a window and presented her letter of credit, asking for a sum of money. The clerk politely scrutinized the letter, turned to examine some files. Then he asked Millinda to wait until he had consulted an official. She was a little surprised; it was only when first she arrived in Paris that she had waited upon formalities of identification for an initial payment.

The clerk returned and asked her to see an official. She walked into an enclosure and was shown a seat. With rare solicitousness the official explained that there were no funds. Millinda's bank was busted. He produced a cablegram from New York, which confirmed the report. Also the item had appeared in newspapers a few days old. But Millinda seldom read the American newspapers published in Paris. She left the bank making an effort to maintain the facade of composure.

With a stack of American Express orders and an assortment of bills, she still retained a feeling of immediate security. She taxied to the office of an American newspaper and procured the copy containing the account of the bank's failure. She shopped to keep her mind normal, ordered liquor, bought neckties and socks for Buster, and some articles at a pharmacist.

When she returned to the hotel, she retired to think in bed. We did fight like a tiger to get money and to hold it. We did fight, Ned and I. It was fighting black and fighting white. They all were like wild hogs but we beat them. And beat the law, too. For the law was white folk's business, protecting big white crooks and hounding little colored racketeers. And when Ned was bounced off, I said: this money is my God, now. I gave my life for it and I can't live without it. But something greater than God has licked me to take it—something mighty powerful like the big black belly of hell.

When Buster came in, Millinda was again her old self. "I've changed my mind about Montmartre. Let's have a party here instead. Go get Lotta and Fanti and tell them to collect some people for a party."

It wasn't difficult on short notice to collect people for a Millinda affair. Lotta did her utmost to get a nice group which would please Millinda and crowd out of their minds the morning's unpleasantness. That evening Millinda's luxurious suite of rooms was animated by a varied congenial collection of persons of different complexions and breeds. From the Congo Vif, Lotta had obtained Kamassa, the Senegalese dancer and her drummer, Ahmed Bubu. Also there was Pucksar, once a favorite Aframerican pianist at Lamour's Cabaret, the high rendezvous of Americans in Paris, but now he was out-of-work. The Baron Belchite was also there. And Fanti had with him the Princess Fanti, his cousin's widow, and Madame Audace and a Parisian couple. Buster had corralled a half a dozen dubious Negroids in Montparnasse, who brought some white friends.

In her boisterous big way Millinda greeted all her guests and told them to make themselves comfortable and gay. Those whom she knew well like Achine Palma, Madame Audace and the Princess Fanti she greeted affectionately and kissed. A large assortment of American and French liquor was arranged on the buffet, and Millinda was as assidious in pouring drinks for the guests as the valet. Pucksar at the piano produced the kind of music which harmonizes with a drinking party, and between snatches of conversation the guests would gang together in groups, clink glasses, shake legs, disperse and come together again.

The *pièce de résistance* of that period was "The Peanut Vendor." With a saucy sweetness Pucksar played it enchantingly. There were few there who could dance the real rhumba, but everyone in his way moved to that melody, deliciously crude like a royal piece of brown sugar cake.

Millinda herself brought a tumblerful of rum and soda over to Pucksar. The Baron Belchite was hovering near the piano and she took him aside: "Aw you nasty man, what made you say that awful thing about black odor to Lotta? Why, her skin is almost as white as yours and nicer, though she may not have had some rotten good-for-nothing noble strain poisoning her blood like yours."

"Please, Madame Millinda, please understand. I said what I did as a compliment to Lotta, the highest compliment. Why, many a high-class woman in Paris would thrill to hear that her odor was sweet to a ma-an. Any white woman would be happy for da-at. And I thought Lotta was becoming to belong to the really civilized minority. But perhaps I was wrong.

"Did you know the grand actress Jolly? Why, her admirers challenged each other to duel to decide who first should take a drink of the water she bathed in. But Lotta is just a dumb girl imagining that she is sophisticated. Frankly with you, Madame Millinda, I don't think it is easy for any Negro person to be sophisticated. If I were a Negro I couldn't be. And that is why I marvel so much at Fanti."

"I guess you're perfectly right," said Millinda.

With hospitable phrases on her lips, seeing that the guests had plenty to drink, Millinda entertained in Paris even as she had in Harlem, and no one there guessed that her mind was heavy with trouble too great to bear.

Pucksar's fingers were flashing a jumbled pattern of hot jazz, when the Princess Fanti moved over by the piano and spoke to him. The princess was supposed to be Spanish. She was a retiring person. Her figure was of a slight, general type. There was nothing markedly Latin in her features. When she was younger she might have been a passably good-looking white woman among many like her. She wore black on almost all occasions, before and since her husband's death. But round her neck she always wore a band of many colored beads, exquisitely wrought, one of the many West African handicraft gifts she had received from her husband.

The colored women of Paris rather resented her being Princess Fanti. They felt that a colored woman should possess that old West African title. For Fanti was not an empty name. It belonged to a powerful house in West Africa. And in Paris it had prestige in certain circles. The deceased Prince Fanti had been a member of scientific societies. He had helped to establish the native West African Museum and was a member of the Board of Directors.

Since his death, his cousin had assumed the responsibility of his widow's affairs. Thus it was part of his duty to take her to some social affairs. But Fanti's set was quite different from that of his dead cousin's and the widow was not home in it. She had asked Pucksar to play a sentimental piece called Song of Harlem in place of the hot jazz stuff.

Achine Palma overheard her and said to Pucksar: "Go on playing that hot piece. Everybody likes it and I'm gonna dance."

"But Madame Fanti asked for the "Song of Harlem," said Pucksar.

"Who cares what *she* asks for," said Achine. "This is not her affair."

"Oh, you needn't be so rude, for I meant nothing at all," said Princess Fanti. "He may play what *you* want."

Prince Fanti approached them and the princess held his arm and said, "I wish you take me home."

"Home, now! Why, it's much too early," said Fanti.

With the princess appropriating Fanti's arm Achine Palma grew angrier. She had definite personal ideas about Fanti, whom she wanted to marry and thus become the first Aframerican princess. Fanti encouraged her by flirtation, but would not commit himself to a promise of marriage. Instinctively Achine regarded the widowed princess as her rival, especially as she had learned that it was a common West African custom for a man to protect a near relative's widow, even by marrying her.

"You may see me home and then return," said Princess Fanti.

"Let the woman go on home by herself," said Achine. "She's not in the African jungle to be afraid. Why, she's carrying on like you were her husband and I wouldn't know."

"Shut up, Achine," said Fanti. "I know that you are the cause of Acuesta wanting to go home. You're just like a crouching leopard, always ready to spring upon somebody."

Millinda saw that something was wrong and came up as the princess said: "Please don't start quarrelling here because of me."

"Now you all must behave," said Millinda, "And Achine, you keep your liplash off people. This is not a cat scratching but a party and I specially want everbody to be happy."

Achine walked away to the buffet muttering: "Princess my eye! She's all folded up like an old rag left under a bathtub."

Millinda in sugary accents prevailed upon Princess Fanti to stay. She found out from Pucksar what started the dispute and told him to play the song.

The "Song of Harlem" was the latest hit. It was written by a Harlem Negro about the time when the popular taste began craving hot jazz or swing music. But the composer could find no publisher willing to take it. There is no Harlem like that in words and music, they said. People don't want that kind of Harlem stuff. The public wants Harlem hot. The composer kept his song. At last a white sympathiser introduced him to the leader of a Negro orchestra. The Negro musician added it to his repertoire and put it over the radio.

The "Song of Harlem" became an immediate success. It came when the tempo of the country had reached a turning point and the public was ready for a different version of Harlem.

So Pucksar played the "Song of Harlem."

> *In Harlem you may find what joy you seek,*
> *But forget not that sorrow lingers there,*
> *Where in the shadows dwell the weak and meek,*
> *Of broken lives whose homes are cold and bare,*
> *Like broken lives of outcasts everywhere,*
>
> *The dusk benignantly enfolds the street,*
> *And gathers Harlem's children to her breast,*
> *And brown madonnas kiss their babies' feet*
> *And tenderly they cradle them to rest:*
> *Oh golden hearts of Harlem in the night,*
> *Oh souls of Harlem searching for the light.*
>
> *In Harlem there is laughter, music, wine,*
> *And beauty bold in strangely haunting eyes,*
> *And also wholesome lives like yours and mine,*
> *And quiet homes wherein the sacred ties*
> *Of love and faith bind humble families.*

The music was an indolent onestep, a kind of pain-in-the-spine shuffle, and out-of-work Pucksar in Paris played it with heart-rending feeling for Harlem. He built up a picture of Harlem there in the room: Lenox Avenue and its fried fish and coffee pots, Eighth Avenue and its vegetable and fish market, Seventh Avenue and its saloons and brown faces against the window panes.

All the guests—Africans, Aframericans, Europeans—swayed to the melody like a cradle rocking to a lullaby. But while the others danced from left to right, the Senegalese dancer moved her head up and down in a kind of subdued interpretation of the primitive Senegalese dance. Achine, captivated and calmed by the music to which she had objected, was rocking in Buster's arms.

But Princess Fanti had sat down in a corner and Millinda had insisted on sitting with her. "I love that song," said the princess, caressing the heavy purple window drapery against her.

"It's pretty," said Millinda, "perhaps you like it because it has a little tango in it."

"No, it's the Negro I like in it more than the hot jazz. It was that kind of Negro I knew. And I found Negro life like that when my husband took me to Africa to present me to the chiefs of his tribe. Everywhere there was that strange undertone of melancholy." She wiped her eyes furtively and said: "Excuse me. I told you I wanted to go home."

"Oh, it's alright," said Millinda, "I understand you. But I didn't know you had been to Africa."

"Oh yes, Prince Fanti took me there two years before his death, so his people could salute me. And he was never right after he returned. I think something happened to him there."

"Did you like Africa?"

"I liked the visit and the people they were so lovely to me. But I wouldn't want to live there."

"Perhaps I should have visited Africa too," said Millinda. "Now it's too late."

"Why too late? Are you going back to New York?"

"I don't know where I'm going—perhaps to hell. Let's drink and forget," said Millinda, getting up.

By two o'clock most of the guests had left. Millinda gave the Senegalese dancer 100 francs, her drummer 50 francs and Pucksar 200 francs. The intimates remained: Lotta Sander and Baron Belchite, Achine Palma, Madame Audace. Prince Fanti had escorted the Princess home and returned. They all sat in the bedroom drinking quietly and gossiping aimlessly. They represented the interesting core of any big party after the casual guests and performers had departed.

Madame Audace was sometimes called *la Premiére* by wits, because of her desire and her achievement in being the first woman of the set in accomplishing certain unconventional things. She was the first aristocrat to accept the Fantis socially as real princes and her act was much appreciated in diplomatic circles. Also she was the first of her set to descend from an airplane in a parachute. And now she was telling of her appearance at a party given by artistic folk for Josephine Baker.

"Ah, yes, she was such a naturally wild creature, carrying on like a mad child as if she were in her Harlem and talking to big influential people as if they were little toys. Oh, it was funny. I was with Fanti, who was introduced as an African Prince, and Josephine said she did not believe that there were African princes who wore no ring in their noses. For when she had to play the part of an African princess, they insisted that she should wear a ring in her nose, because African royalty wore rings in their noses, by which they were led. All Europeans know that. I gave a special interview of the party, to which they signed my name and paid me 5000 francs. I gave all of it to charity. Yes, I like to get all the new sensations first, when they are fresh."

Said Achine: "I've always wondered why Princess Fanti does not wear a ring in *her* nose, since she is not authentic royalty and so ordinary as a person, she might at least do something to make herself distinctive."

They all laughed and Prince Fanti said: "No one would think of saying that but you, Achine. You got the blood of the African leopard in you."

Millinda had left the room, and the talk went on mainly between Audace and Achine. "I'm not naturally mean," said Achine, "but that Princess Fanti makes me feel real evil. I'm colored, after all, and I like to see my people shine. You don't pick up a real African prince every day, so she could at least carry herself like a real princess."

"Oh, I think she does it pretty well, considering the class she comes from," said Madame Audace.

"Oh, I don't think class counts," said Achine. After all, she was American, her mother was a cook. And nobody knew the real source of the income on which she lived abroad. It was rumored that she had been the youthful housekeeper of her mother's aged employer, who had eluded his relatives and lived abroad, so that a colored girl might continue as his housekeeper.

"Don't be too jealous, Achine," said Lotta, "some day you may get that title and know how to use it." Aware of Achine's ambition she winked at Fanti.

"And you bet I'd use it right," said Achine. "If I were married to a prince and living in Paris, why I'd make my title talk and sing in my clothes and my style."

Loud shrieks penetrated into the room. It was Millinda's voice: "Lawd, Lawdy! Buster, I'm burning up. Oh Buster, Fire, Lawd, Fire!"

They rushed into the bathroom and found Millinda fallen backwards into the tub and screaming hell-fire. Buster pulled her up and held her: "What is it? What's the matter?"

"Oh, I'm burning up!" she screamed. "Fire inside a me! Doggone it all! God damn you all! Fire, Lawd, Fire!" She struggled wildly, but Buster held her tightly and the women helping, carried her into the bedroom. Fanti had rushed out to find a doctor. But Millinda's struggling grew feebler, her screaming fell to a low moan and she was merely twitching. Long before Fanti returned, she was dead.

Lotta and Achine were half paralysed by fright. But Madame Audace arranged Millinda's clothes and straightened her out on the bed and lit a cigarette. Back in the bathroom Buster glanced around as if he were looking for the strange swift assassin. He found only an empty bottle. Millinda had poisoned herself.

32

5

BUSTER'S BACK

Buster returned to New York quietly, alone. After months of precarious existence abroad, impulsively he made up his mind to return and took leave of Lotta Sander and her Nordic baron, Achine Palma and her black prince and Marie Audace and her bohemian aristocrats.

Buster was a different person from the gay devil of a black buck, who was formerly a sheik of Harlem. For Millinda's suicide, suddenly cutting him adrift abroad, had so scared his spirit out of him that now he was afraid of his own shadow. He was like an underworldling living arrogantly a clandestine existence, boldly flouting the instinctive ideas of common conduct, who at last was trapped in the net of the law, and after being third-degreed, physically or psychically, could never again regain his egoistic spirit of self-confidence.

From down in the deep South, Buster had come up to the North, making long stops on the way in Atlanta, in St. Louis and Chicago. He had done all sorts of things imaginable which an unschooled, determined black boy might do to keep going along with the maelstrom of American life. Buster ran errands, washed cars, helped drive them, and delivered groceries, peeled vegetables, washed dishes, watered gardens, beat rugs and made beds. He was likeable, good at making contacts and friends.

When he landed in New York he picked up acquaintances who introduced him to the Bing Bang Club, which was situated in a basement in 133rd Street, between Fifth and Lenox Avenues, which was then known as the Jungle Block. In the last years of Prohibition this club changed its name to King Kong. The club dealt in little clandestine activities, such as cards, reefers, numbers and bootleg liquor. It was the mean knockout this liquor possessed which gave the club its new name, the King Kong.

Buster stuck to the club and through it found a means of subsistence. There was a small lunch counter and if its boss had to leave it awhile, Buster would lend his hand. If the billiard marker had to absent himself a moment, Buster would take his place and he even helped the shine boy.

Meanwhile Buster kept his eyes and ears alert. He visited other clubs, attended dances and met many girls. He was invited to affairs over beyond Eighth Avenue up on Edgecombe and St. Nicholas Avenue where the more refined Harlemites were endeavoring to make a stand against the masses. Buster possessed splendid aplomb and was equally liked in refined as with rough circles.

He introduced some members of the refined fast set to the King Kong, and they enjoyed the atmosphere. The manager of the King Kong made Buster his assistant. All this happened at precisely that period when that ultra-sophisticated fringe of white society—literati, artists and aesthetes—were discovering Harlem. At first their contacts had been limited to the burgeoning little group of writers and artists.

And so from the shadows of the black belt Buster emerged with an inimitable adaptability; he pushed forward as the up and coming young man of Harlem. He was an invaluable asset to white and also black sophisticates, acting as a safe bridge between Harlem high and low.

As Millinda Rose was the woman of the moment in Harlem, her meeting Buster was inevitable. The social gulf between a successful numbers queen and and a King-Konger is wide enough, even in the small territory of Harlem, but aided by the speakeasy tolerance of the times and the broadmindedness of the white sophisticates, the gulf was easily bridged.

Also, in spite of its kings and queens and controllers, accoutred in secret and gaudy high places, the numbers game remains the most democratic institution in Harlem. More than the saloon or the church, it has brought people together in friendly fellowship. No person of any strata of Harlem society is offended, when a collector asks if he would like to play a number. Any Harlemite meeting another, who is a total stranger, and asking, ''What is the number today?'' is certain of a civil answer.

The fascinating numbers game contributed to broader contacts, larger views, mellow ideas and general dreams of wonderful castles in Spain.

Many of the white friends of Harlem became interested in playing the game after meeting with Millinda. Just for the fun of it, they said, or perhaps they imagined there was real black magic inherent in those numbers that were dreamed and manipulated with such fetish ritual by the Negroes. Rapidly also the contagion of playing numbers was spreading among the whites who were doing legitimate business in Harlem.

When Buster went abroad with Millinda, a Hoover presided over the nation. When he returned, it was under the rule of a Roosevelt. The radical changes, in Harlem at least, enormously struck his eye. The saloons, which once stood like abandoned freight cars on the corners, were ablaze with light and gay with modern furnishings and mechanized music, a sharp contrast to the nights when the shuttered windows and doors were like pictures turned to the wall and showing nothing but the gray canvas.

Soon all of Harlem that belonged to Millinda's set, more or less, and especially those interested in the manner of her death, were excited that Buster was back. Everybody was eager for firsthand details of the suicide. But Buster was not quick to gossip about the tragedy. He was haunted by Millinda's last party and attended very few of the parties to which he was invited.

More than anything, Buster desired to break the old pattern of his life and find a regular job. But he discovered that it was no easy thing for one to climb out of the groove in which he has been accustomed to take existence for granted.

A good job was difficult to land. The bloated bodies of black rackets were reduced to skin and bones. Repeal had taken adventure and hot money out of the Prohibition racket. And the magic had vanished from the numbers game. Federal and municipal investigators had crippled the plan of playing. Instead of the Stock Exchange, the playing numbers were derived from the race-track returns. Local hits or winnings were infrequent and small. No more was Harlem mesmerised by dreams of making its fortune from fantastic financial figures. Buster met bankers and controllers on the avenue, their pompous big bellies sagging, their clothing old and worn. Formerly they rode round Harlem in powerful cars with liveried chauffeurs.

One afternoon he called on Jerry Batty who used to be inconspicuously somewhere in the rear ranks of Millinda's set. Batty was the former owner of a hotel mainly for transients and which was also a rendezvous for colored and white. It was closed during the Seabury investigations. Recently he had tried to establish another hotel on similar lines, but it was a failure. The changing times called for a different kind of business. However Batty still possessed the means to live fairly comfortably.

Batty had invited Buster to drop in sometime for a talk. And Buster had chosen the time when he felt sorely in need of a friendly word. Batty, stocky, round-shouldered, dark-brown and bald in the front, with his middle like a puncheon, was wrapped in a green dressing gown and wearing Japanese straw slippers. He was very affable and full of advice. ''Buster-boy, what are you doing with yourself? You got a big asset, if you will spin around and put it to use instead of standing still. I got a good idea you can use. All those white folks what useta fool around Millinda and liked you—where are they?''

"Guess they're all scattered around and most of them broke like me.''

"You're crazy if you think so. White folks can never be broke like niggers. You see, it's like this: Life is like a loaf of bread and niggers nevah did have much more'n the crumbs what the white folks gived them anyway. But now you see the white folks done stop selling bread whole like it always was and like it always should be. For the white folks are fools of inventions. So now they sells the bread already sliced to suit white folks' thin lips and there're no crumbs left for niggers. But the white folks don't go hungry, because they makes the bread. Now you see and understand.'' Batty rubbed his hands together, laughed, very pleased with his wit.

"That don't mean anything. I know plenty of hungry white folks,'' said Buster.

"But not like niggers, I tell you, brother. If white folks go hungry it's because they like to experiment too much with all their ballyhoo about diet and vitamins, all het up in their head and forgetting the great big maw, just as I say how they start slicing the bread and not thinking a goddam about us who depend on the crumbs.

"But as I started to say, I got an idea for you. And it's this: You can bring the white folks back to Harlem like the way they useta come around Millinda. You're the onliest man can do it. You black is true, but you's a handsome one and most personal with personality. And white folks like a straight black nigger, when he is alright. That I know from experience. If you can bring the white folks back to Harlem again and keep them interested, you can make a fortune. You—''

"There are more white people in Harlem than ever before,'' said Buster.

"Them reds and those cheap nigger-busting racketeers? Them's the ones that scares away the real white folks. Top class white folks don't like that kind. They ruined mah place and and if evah I stahts another I won't have'm, no sir. No nice white ladies like to sit up in a cabaret in Harlem and watch their cheap sistahs chasing after niggers.''

"I don't see why they should object,'' said Buster, "when those same women go every place downtown.''

"They object because it makes them feel cheap among the niggers. With all your experience you don't know the white folks psychologically. Downtown they are among their own kind. They come to Harlem for something different. But now in Harlem the white racketeers cater to a cheap white crowd and the niggers with a little money spend it all. Whereas before the niggers made all the money.''

"Different times make different people. That's how it appears to me,'' said Buster. "I can't do what Millinda did. She attracted white folks with money because she had money. That alone was her big drawing card—a colored woman playing high society like a white woman. Beside, her nature was sweet as sugar. I heard white people say she had the real black magic. But brother, I can't manufacture that kind of thing. I ain't got'em.''

"You got a bigger thing than any nigger in Harlem, if you knew how to use it instead of just fiddling around,'' said Batty. "What kind of job do you expect to find? Everybody is on relief.''

Buster yawned. Batty had not even offered a drink. And even more than a drink, he craved a cigarette. He had not smoked all day. His lips twitched, his palate itched. And as he was endeavoring to give up the luxury of cigarettes, the desire was more acute. Batty extracted a cigarette from the pocket of his dressing gown and lit it. "Give me one, old man,'' said Buster.

"Damn! I'm sorry. It was the last one, I just found it in my pocket by accident.''

Buster was tortured, "Well, gimme a glass of water, then.'' He felt he must have something. Batty went back down the long corridor to the kitchen.

Observing an ornament, shaped like a small tom-tom painted in bright colors, sitting on a stand near Batty's chair, Buster got up to examine it. Lifting the lid Buster found the receptacle half full of cigarettes. "Good God!'' he cried, rubbing his eyes to make sure they had not deceived him. He heard Batty coming back and quickly put back the cover.

Buster gulped the glass of water. "Thirsty, eh, want some more?'' said Batty.

"Yes,'' said Buster, "I'll take another glass.'' As Batty walked down the corridor again, Buster removed the lid and filled his pockets with the cigarettes. "What made me hesitate at first?'' he said. "That mean barrel-bottom back-scuttler!'' He merely tasted the second glass of water when Batty returned, and, setting it down, he picked up his hat and said: "Good-bye Batty, I'll dig you again soon.''

6

KING KONG

Walking along Harlem's Fifth Avenue one evening, Buster was accosted by an old King-Konger. They had not met for many years. The King-Konger had quit the old rendez-vous joint before Buster and now was married and the father of three children. He was working as a subway porter downtown and was very quiet and always sober now. In the *Harlem Nugget* he had noticed Buster's photograph and heard mention of him as a black socialite. Also he had read about his traveling abroad.

They talked about Harlem of yesterday and today. The porter complimented Buster on his appearance remarking that he looked as "fresh as a rose." Buster said, "You look fine, too," but he did not mean it. The porter appeared tired, overworked. Looking at him, Buster felt no regret that he hadn't continued working as a porter. The porter said that his first son was a smart boy and going to junior high school. Well that was real compensation for cleaning a subway station all one's life, thought Buster and he said, "That's fine. Guess you'll train him to be a professor."

"I don't think so. He's crazy about mail carriers and wants to work in the post office."

The King Kong club had changed managers many times and had moved from the Jungle Block to Seventh Avenue, where it was located in a basement. "Suppose we give it the once-over," said the porter. "I haven't been there since I left it in the jungle and don't imagine I know a soul there."

"And I haven't been there in years," said Buster.

They walked over to Seventh Avenue. The suggestion seemed to take hold of Buster and carry him along, more than the porter, whom he found uninteresting. They got into the club easily. It was a broad basement divided into two compartments. In the front one, which was the larger, the tables were covered with figured oil cloth. There was a little lunch counter and a few cigar boxes and cigarettes in a shelf. Also there was an old piano and beside it a mechanized player. In the rear room there was a pool table, a couple of old couches and small tables.

The members were youths. Five of them were playing pool in the rear room. The others played cards. All of them wore short brown leather coats. Not all of them drank hooch. But all of them smoked reefers (the marijuana weed), the manager supplying the cigarettes. The manager was a stout dark man, standing solidly on his feet. He was formerly a female impersonator of the rough burlesque type and had delighted the hard-boiled patrons of colored cabarets from San Francisco to New York. The big scene of his act used to be a parody of congenitally effeminate female impersonators.

The porter introduced himself to the manager and presented Buster. "Glad you all dropped in to look us over," said the manager and to Buster, "I know a thousand people in Harlem who claim to know you, yet we never did meet."

"I guess more people know me than I know mahself," said Buster.

"Yeah man, you said it, I've heard a ton of tales about you."

"Good or bad?"

"I wasn't unfavorably depressed, but what difference would that make to you? I prefer niggers dishing dirt about me than saying nothing at all. It is bettah to be remembered than forgotten, brother, especially if you're a business man as you and I is."

The manager stood a coca-cola bottle of liquor on the table and said: "This is on the house for the honorable members." This special bootleg was sold at 25 cents a bottle, which could fill up five whisky glasses. The porter tasted it and said: "This is undertaker's rot-gut." Buster swallowed his glass and made a face as if fire had burned his gullet. "But why do people drink this stuff? Bootleg was better during Prohibition."

"Sure it was, for the big dealers were in the racket making and smuggling good liquor. But now they're in regular business again, they're fighting the bootleggers. You can't get no good whisky for 5 cents."

"I'd sooner drink nothing," said Buster.

"The niggers on relief can't afford good liquor," said the porter. "And they're them folks afflicted with a Prohibition hangover who drink hooch like you drink medicine. They won't touch good liquor. What gets me is the young kids like these here drinking the stuff. They drink it because it's cheap and to feel cockish, just like they prefer reefers to cigarettes. When I see them in a place like this, I think of my own boy and I feel wild."

"But your kid is too young," said Buster.

"Brother, theah's nothing too young for this hole of Harlem. I works and my wife works. And young boys are like womens. You can nevah tell what tricks they're up to."

The porter ordered a bottle of the camouflaged coca-cola. "I've got to order one since the manager treated us," he said.

An old man came in shuffling and stooping as if some trouble had bent his back. He looked like a weak stick upon which the loose bag of a gray-brown suit was carelessly hung. His face was like a crumpled piece of brown paper. He spoke to nobody. He shuffled up to the counter, paid a quarter for a coca-cola bottle of hooch and began drinking alone.

A lad came from the rear room and put a coin in the nickelodeon. As the music started he held his leather coat behind with his left hand and began a strange rearing prancing. The old man dropped his head to the counter as if he had fallen asleep. The manager viciously thumbed him in his side. The old fellow got his head up and looked around hazily. Suddenly he said: "I'll be jitterbugged" and started shuffling over to Buster's table, looking like an old suit hanging on a rack which was being pushed out of the way. He palmed Buster's shoulder and cried: "Why, if it ain't the big Buster himself. I ain't nevah set eyes on you sence I heared you done crash the big gates. Why, don't you remember me?"

"Sure I do," said Buster, "How're you, pap?" But although he did not easily forget faces he could not recall this man, who also was convinced that Buster did not remember him.

"You just don't remember me, tops. You've forgotten Spareribs Duke who runned the lunch counter when you first stahted coming 'round to the Bing Bang!"

"Oh yes," said Buster. "Gee! How could I have forgot!"

"Well, ef you even fohgits me, you sho should remember mah spareribs."

Buster smiled, but it was inwardly uncomfortable, remembering the many free spareribs the Duke had fed him, and now meeting him after all these years broken in body and and evidently also in need.

"Well, say something," said Duke, "or blow your top and make you' action talk instead."

"That's okay, Duke. Another time. I think you got enough."

"Lookeheah, big shot, in this heah joint we don't wanta hear no bellyache blues. I knows when ah got enough. It's my business ef I want to booze tell ahm paralyzed. What's wrong wif you? Don't tell me you're plumb broke like all the rest of the big shots."

The leather-coated lads, strangely uneasy, nerves twitching from the effects of the reefers, crowded round. They were highly amused by Spareribs Duke, who was everybody's joke, now making a fool of one Big Shot.

Buster wished that he had never gone to the club. He was confused and bungled badly: "I'm okay, pals. I'll treat the gang some other time. I'm not exactly broke, but sometimes a fellow is short. You understand." They all laughed loudly understandingly.

"Don't hand us that stuff, for we ain't taking," said Old Duke. "Don't play us cheap. Lawd, lawdiness, after flying so high in black-and-white sasiety, you're right back heah like the rest of us wif—*nothing*."

Duke shuffled back from the table and struck a stiff theatrical pose; he began a tap strut sticking to one spot and singsonging: "Stepping high and falling low; stepping high and falling low." The boys rhythmically clapped their hands and jigged around him, the hot drug making them feel as if they were high up in the air. As if she had broken out of some secret place, a stout little black girl shot wildly into the room dancing around the group, bouncing with elastic enthusiasm like a rubber ball among the men. The nickel music spun roaring and flashing like a bawdy dispute among them. The pungent odor of reefers hung in the smoke like heavy thunder in a storm.

Buster felt the dancing like a merciless pounding in his back. And in reality the pivot of the movement was his back. Systematically the girl broke away from the ring followed by the fellows and stamped up behind him laughing at his back. Then they danced away to reform the ring and returned again. Suddenly the Duke started barking and extending his head like a hound. And at one moment when his voice rose to a high pitch as if it would pop out of him like a bullet, the Duke pranced and leaped as if he were going to hit the ceiling and fell with a thud sprawling upon his back.

Frightened, Buster and the porter jumped up. But the manager reassured them: "He ain't dead. It's the reefers. Someathem laughs till they faint, some bawl like a baby and someathem bark like a dog. Some dance all the time and sometimes imagine they're animals and gits down on them knees and crawls."

Buster seized the opportunity to get out of the place. He walked along Seventh Avenue. He felt that some persons seemed to be curiously excited by him as he passed by. Many laughed mockingly. "Gawd!" he said, "I feel as if all of Harlem knows that I am broke." He dreaded going by the Bamboo Pole cabaret, in front of which stood a gang of men in a gaudy glow of light. Perhaps there were acquaintances among them. As he approached he felt happy there was none. But as he went by, a blast of laughter struck him like a backside kick. "The devil's doings!" said Buster, "What can those sons-o' guns know about me?" He glanced back and saw two of the gang throwing an act. One fellow danced around and palming the other in face said: "You're a bum!" "Yeah," said the other, palming him back, "and you are beat." The gang roared with amusement.

Buster was non-plussed and said: "Anyway, Harlem got the stuff alright, with the niggers frisking and loud-laughing as high as the sky." In his room he discovered the secret of the unusual hilarity. Upon taking off his coat he found pinned in the middle a sheet of paper upon which was written in a large hand: BUM-BEAT.

Buster raved with rage: "The reefer rats, those Harlem snakes! I'll show'm I'm no bum. I'm not yet beat. Yes, I will show'm."

7
CHANGE OF ADDRESS

Buster inhabited a little room overlooking the elevated tracks high up towards the ending of Eighth Avenue. His rendezvous was a candy store, which was a front for the numbers game. In the rear the proprietor reserved a room for card and dice players—persons who were in his confidence—and thus added a little to the diminishing profits of the numbers game. All the players belonged to fraternal orders and the majority were Elks.

In his determination to cut loose from his past, Buster had joined one of the Elks' lodges. His proselytising brothers had sold him the Elks as the livest order among Negroes. The members of his lodge were all humble working men, porters, elevator runners, chauffeurs and a very few who had no apparent means of existence. These men lived on a lower level than the numbers kings and queens and others who set the fast pace of Aframerican society. Also they were far removed from the King-Kongites and tea-hounds of the reefer joints. They and their women were the types who make the backbone of the African Methodist and Baptist churches. But it was they, too, who contributed liberally to the golden treasury of the numbers kings even as they did to the coffers of the churches.

They were friendly fraternal games, which were played in the rear of the candy store. Buster won often. Somehow, he managed to live. Frugal living. But he felt better in these men's company than among the King-Kongers and even happier (now that he was able to take stock of them) than among the smart set.

Some of Buster's new friends thought that he would make a good manager of a club. Buster thought so, too. He had once been a master of ceremonies in a cabaret and aspired to that role again. But the cabaret

43

business (once entirely in the hands of colored caterers) was not so good in Harlem since white competitors had entered the field. The best equipped places were owned by whites and the trade went there.

One late morning, Buster was making his breakfast, the coffee bubbling and filling the small room with a delicious odor, when a broad brown woman barged in on him. Her face was friendly and sweet as a homemade apple pie.

"Bless mah soul, so this heah birdcage is the place," she said, "an' it sho could take an honest-to-goodness cleaning all ovah."

"Well, bless mah soul, mahself," said Buster, catching the happy spirit of the woman, "and who told you that I was under the liability of living here?"

"A lil stool pigeon of which theah's as many as niggers in Harlem. But you haven't yet said youse glad to see me."

"Do I need to? Which is better? To see it in my eyes or to hear it in my mouth?"

"Bofem good."

The visitor, Charlotte Pointer, was formerly Millinda's cook. She was working for Millinda when Buster appeared on the scene. She had felt a motherly affection for the tall black youngster, showing more interest in him than the other hangers-on, most of whom she despised. Often when she had prepared an especially fine dish of black-eyed peas and baked lamb or fried chicken and sugared yam, she said to Millinda: "I am cooking something nice for you and Mister Souf."

She had left Millinda's service long before the crisis in the numbers game, but had remained sentimental about her service with Millinda. For it was through it that she had obtained a job in a little hotel downtown, which she still held. A visitor to Millinda's had become ecstatic over Charlotte's cooking: her sugared yam and black-eyed peas and lima beans, and lick-your-fingers fried chicken and her delicious gravy. And he had recommended Charlotte to the manager of the little hotel featuring Southern cooking. Charlotte had worked there ever since.

"You ain't even got a chair to set on, m-m-m!" Charlotte rolled her eyes and her head. (The electric stove was sitting on the rickety old chair.) She turned down the spread of the unmade bed and sat. "Buster, what kinda joint is thiseah? It needs a powerful scrubbing and indeed a lot of disaffection."

"Things are different," said Buster.

"You telling me? How otherwise could you be staying in a place like this? Harlem is almost like a can a cinders now. The Depression got the niggers straight in the neck. And all the trifling no-count rag-cutters ain't worf no more than the raggedy hole in the seat of their pants and the soles of their shoes. But you're different, Buster. Even ef you were a little wrong sometimes, you were always regular, just like Millinda.''

Charlotte's voice broke into a kind of whimper: "I sure did cry my heart sick unto breaking when I heared about her moving death that sudden way. Tell me the truth, Buster, did she really throw a grand suicide pahty?''

Charlotte's sentimental inquisitiveness did not offend Buster. He had always remembered her motherly interest in Millinda. Often in his own presence she warned Millinda about the hangers-on and back-biters of the fast set. And Millinda listened to Charlotte, sometimes impatiently, but nevertheless, she would listen. But if one of the pace-makers dared to give her advice like Charlotte, Millinda would jump down that person's throat.

So Buster loosened up and told Charlotte everything. And after telling about Millinda and her strange passing, he talked about himself abroad, trying to live by his wits like Lotta Sander, sometimes teaming up with her. Full of sympathy, Charlotte listened to Buster's talking about himself and telling of his determination now to do something different.

And straightly she told him that if he really wanted to do something different, he would have to quit the frowzy environment of Eighth Avenue. She herself lived above the lower Harlem level up on St. Nicholas Avenue. She invited Buster to come up to dinner when she got her free day.

That day of the dinner had some surprises for Buster. He was surprised by the familiar look of Charlotte's apartment, which was furnished something like Millinda's former apartment. The heavy chairs were covered with the same kind of flowered chintz and the long window curtains were the same material. Millinda had liked pretty Italianate statuettes; Charlotte had three of them ornamenting the corners of her living room.

Charlotte's husband was crippled and prematurely gray. He could barely hobble about on crutches. Also there was a lodger, a demure brown girl named Oleander Powers. She was having dinner with Charlotte and Buster. In the spacious dining room, there was a modernistic buffet decorated with a fine set of Japanese dishes, which reminded Buster of a favorite set of Millinda's. It was a fat dinner of tomato soup, sugar-cured ham and fried chicken with rice, yams and string beans. Charlotte piled plenty on Buster's plate. And his eager appetite showed he had not for a long time tasted such good food.

"Loosen yoh belt and fill up,'' said Charlotte. "When I cooks mah food I like it appreciated by folks who'm used to good things. Down at mah hotel I gits moh compliments than I can digest. And I knows ah'm tops and no matter what happens to poh niggers I'se all right so long as white folks appreciate good down-home cooking.''

"That's plenty true," said Buster. "Way back in the days when I wrastled with pots and pans in the white folks' hotel, the cook used to croon when she was in a good mood:

To keep always in the white folks grace,
Chilluns!
You must know how to feed their face,
Chilluns!

"Chilluns is right, black and white," said Charlotte. "And blessed are the feeders, says I, for life is mostly big moufs."

Oleander was extremely reticent and most wistful. She worked occasionally as a maid, although she had finished a commercial high school and was a competent stenographer. But she could not find a white-collar job. One drawback was she did not know the important people in Harlem who could help her get a white-collar job. Also she was not a member of any of the smart social clubs.

"And what will the little mouths like me do?" she essayed.

"Feed the big moufs, chile and keep feeding," said Charlotte.

After dinner, Oleander said she would clean up the kitchen alone as Charlotte had done all the cooking. Charlotte showed Buster the apartment. There was a small unoccupied room, in which was stored old clothes, hat boxes, lamps and like things. Buster asked why it was not rented. Charlotte said she had decided to have one lodger only. "Harlem is jest like a mighty big and cheap over-crowded boding house with ehvybody renting rooms. There is no family life like it is down home. So I says when I moved up heah with mah old man, I'd try to make a home to live in, cos I hed a good job of couhse."

"I don't blame you," said Buster, "Harlem could stand a lot more space. We're piled upon one another like potatoes in a sack, up here in Harlem."

"I'll fix up that there little room as a special favor for you, ef you wants it," said Charlotte, "You'll have an address anyhow, which you sure need to get on you' feet again and you kain't have an address on the Eighth Avenue."

"But I don't have money for Sugar Hill rent."

"You will pay me when you make some. I know you got the stuff in you to make it. You'll get there. But you got to staht right to get back into the swing of Harlem again."

"Charlotte, I don't want to live the same way again."

"Now, you think you telling me something. I know you don't or else you wouldn't be bunking down there on Eighth Avenue. But if you gwineta do some'n different, it'll be some'n halfways decent, won't it? And you kain't do nothing without a decent address."

"I guess you're right about that."

"I know it. You ain't in the same class as them trifling panhandling rug-cutters who useta sponge on Millinda. And because you was her choice, I knew there was something to you. For all her cutting up Millinda was no or'nary woman to like an or'nary man. She was the one nigger woman I ever worked for, because there was class to her. You think it ovah and decide."

So Buster moved up on the exclusive hill of Harlem. But change of address did not produce immediate results. He tried for new contacts and often rubbed shoulders with former acquaintances of the smart set, most of them like himself out of luck, derelicts hanging on to the bars of gin mills. Of the many things suggested to him, the most practicable was the management of a contemplated new cabaret. The manager of the candy store and clandestine auxiliaries had some money saved and was planning to break into the legitimate liquor business with a new cabaret. He was already sure of support for the new venture because of his faithful following among the Elks and other steady customers of his backroom activities. Buster had been mentioned as a possible master of ceremonies, and everybody thought he was just the man for the job. However, it would be a few months yet before the candy store could be transformed to accommodate the new venture.

Charlotte encouraged Buster. "Harlem isn't what it used to be, but you'll get a break. The niggers am still spending a lot of money, but only the preachers and the white folks getting it."

Buster found time from his little activities to be kind to Mr. Poynter, Charlotte's husband. Sometimes he took him down in the elevator and helped him across the street to the park to sit out in the air awhile. And sometimes he read to him interesting items from the newspaper as he sat humbly in his corner by the radiator in the front room.

Meanwhile, Charlotte was thinking out a plan that she thought might help Buster and decided upon a surprise party. She had thought that it might mean something for Buster if she could get together some of the more interesting persons who formerly made up Millinda's set to come to a party for him. So secretly she had gone about making contacts with persons, some of whom she had not seen in five years.

47

Charlotte had no difficulty finding the right people to come to her party. Many of them still reminisced in their sentimental moments about the appetite-teasing fried chicken she served in the past for Millinda's affairs. Charlotte was respectable and solidly fixed enough to have at her home members of Harlem society, even though she did not belong to it. She was not just an ordinary cook; her job downtown put her on par with successful colored caterers. And in the polite circles of Harlem she was referred to as a lady chef.

The party was fixed for Charlotte's free day. She had arranged for Oleander to get Buster to take her to a movie show and contrived to keep him away from the house until late in the evening.

Oleander and Buster went to a picture theater in 125th street. She was a nice girl with an attractive warm maroon complexion. She was neatly formed and shapely as a bluebell. And she was extremely romantic. She had come to New York from a near Western state to finish her education. Her father was a preacher and her ways indicated her leaning to ritualistic ideals. She was possessed by the idea of Negro progress and rather indiscriminately held in reverence the outstanding personalities of the colored group. She was hypercritical of black Harlem and the antics of the fast set and often said that Harlem could do much more substantial things with its great opportunities.

Oleander and Buster sat back in the rear of the little theater. The film was a romantic love story. During the unfolding of a very sentimental episode, Buster slid his arm around her waist and pressed her to him. Reacting to the pressure she tried to ease away, but impulsively he planted a kiss on her mouth. She gave up resistance and when he removed his mouth said: "Did you have enough?"

Buster was embarrassed and after a little hesitation said: "Do you think I have?"

"That didn't answer my question."

"Guess I made you angry. I'm sorry if I did."

"Don't apologize, because I don't intend to say, 'You belong to me now'."

"Suppose I wanted to say that first, being the male."

"Say what?"

"That you belong to me or perhaps 'I love you.'"

"What kind of love? Love on relief?"

"Oh, Lord, you did hit the mark then," Buster laughed.

"Did it hurt?"

"Well, I'm still laughing," said Buster. "It didn't do more than cancel our feelings and make us friends."

"Let's shake friendly hands then?" said Oleander.

When they got back home, Charlotte's front room was animated with guests. Buster knew some of them. Jerry Batty was the first to say hello. And there was Patsinette Smythe, a house decorator, who had earned good money decorating Millinda's apartment and as advisory aide on entertaining; Tillie Ashmead, a light-complexioned school-teacher, also belonging to Millinda's set; Gypsy Nilequeen, President of the Palace of Beauty, who was Harlem's prominent beautician and a stout blue-black beauty herself; Bibba Prentice, formerly a controller of the numbers game who worked for Millinda and who still had a good job working for an Italian numbers banker, whom she had brought to the party: he appeared rather uncomfortable. Also there were Homer Lake, a Harlem politician, Tucker Kader, a tall, light-complexioned and good-looking youngster, who apparently was to some dame what Buster had been to Millinda and who was also one of the rare ones of that species still moving in Harlem society. And also there was Baldwin Hatcher, white. It was Hatcher who had recommended Charlotte to that job in the hotel downtown. And it was he, too, who first presented Millinda in a metropolitan newspaper as hostess of Harlem.

Buster was angry when he saw that Charlotte had trapped him into a party. He thought perhaps Charlotte was trying to show off because he was staying at her house. Charlotte observed his confused look and said in his ear: "I thought up this heah surprise to make you meet ole friends and maybe find a way to something new. It's a lil nothing ef we kin do something to help you whiles youse looking out for you'self."

"Okay, Charlotte," Buster patted her shoulder affectionately. He realized that she was doing what she considered the best thing for him and that he should not be ungrateful.

"Come back in the dining room and have a good stiff drink," she said. Patsinette Smythe captured Buster's arm and went along with them.

The modernistic buffet was thickly decorated with many bottles of Seagrams, Calvert's, Mount Vernon, gin, wine, ginger ale and club soda. "H'm, you're a grand gal, Charlotte," said Patsinette, "serving all that real good liquor."

"I want you all here to drink good liquor and see that youse drinking it," said Charlotte, "because I hear that some of the best people of Harlem are still serving hooch at their pahties, though they buy good liquor for their own use."

"That's honest truth," said Patsinette, "and especially those benefit parties. Some of them even put the stuff in regular store bottles to fool you. I tell you I don't drink any more of those camouflage cocktails, for good alcohol is high and hard to get, and the bootleg now is deadly.''

Oleander came in with a tray to get some drinks, followed by Tucker Kader. The radio was playing. ''Let's go up front and dance,'' said Patsinette, leading Buster by the hand.

''Why have you been avoiding everybody ever since your return?'' asked Patsinette.

''It wasn't me doing the avoiding so much as you-all,'' said Buster.

''Oh go on!'' Patsinette twisted through the dance like a snake, working her shoulders up and down. ''I'm not an avoiding type of woman and I've always wanted you. Perhaps you didn't want to know it, but Millinda sure did.''

Buster laughed. The radio stopped and Charlotte was right at their elbow with a trayful of drinks. Tucker Kader made a neat bow to the tray and lifted off a glass.

''Charlotte,'' said Patsinette, taking one, ''you're as good as your liquor.''

''Help you'self all you want, mah chilluns,'' said Charlotte, ''and drink to Buster's success.''

Six persons were sitting on the long couch with Gypsy Nilequeen regally beaming in the center. ''This is as fine as a Millinda party,'' she said, ''excepting there are no society white folks.''

Said Miss Ashmead: ''Although I socialize a lot with my friends downtown, I do miss the nice white people coming to Harlem like they used to when Millinda was here. The atmosphere in Harlem was more refined then.''

A young girl standing before the couch and leaning on Tucker Kader said: ''Why can't some of you others carry on like Millinda? You could all get together.''

''You can't do it all together,'' said Bibba Prentice. ''It always takes one person to start something big and keep it going the way Millinda did. Millinda made her money work like magic, and society whites specially liked her. Harlem was wild about her ways, for if there's anything can turn colored folks' heads it's big money and white skin.''

''You mean white skin with class to it,'' said Miss Ashmead, with a sly glance at Baldwin Hatcher, who was sitting by a window on the other side of the room and talking to Buster.

Charlotte bustled over to them with two glasses of scotch and soda.

Not too loudly, so Baldwin Hatcher could not hear, Tucker Kader said: ''There are more reasons, too, why nice white folks don't come to

Harlem anymore. It's because they were gypped so often at some of those house parties. The women had their bags rifled, and some of the men lost their expensive overcoats."

Batty was sitting next to Bibba Prentice, and there was a curiously embarrassing expression in his face as he said: "You can't blame Harlem for that. White people also get robbed at parties in the best homes downtown. That's why there are always detectives at them big parties."

Patsinette crossed over to Baldwin Hatcher and Buster and, sitting between them, said: "This is a little like old times, eh? A really nice party."

The radio was turned on, and Tillie Ashmead beckoned Buster to dance. Buster was famed as one of the best dancers in Harlem during the latter hectic high days of Prohibition. Women often said that they were carried away by his feet. He swung to rhythm expertly. He desired to help make the party a success for Charlotte as much as she had tried to make it a success for him. He was never an affectionate type, but he felt Charlotte closer than his mother, although he had never experienced much mother-love, never having had any real home life. He had never given affection to women, and he had never expected affection. But of all he had met at home and abroad, not one could compare with Charlotte.

Buster had made himself agreeable to everybody, excepting Batty, whom he had avoided. But Batty was filling up his barrel with that good liquor and was heavily rolling around the room, especially after Patsinette Smythe, with whom he had had a brief hectic love affair in the days of Millinda's glory. Patsinette had not found white Baldwin Hatcher as entertaining as other downtowners she had met in Harlem. He leaned a little too much over to the serious view of things. So she had left his side ostensibly to replenish her glass, but she did not return. She was waiting at the other end of the room to get Buster after the radio dance.

But as she got Buster in a corner, Batty rolled up to them: "Well, sistah, you been high-hatting me all evening, so I guess I can't talk to you no more."

"Patsinette can never be high-hat, Mr. Batty." She agitated her shoulders in her peculiar way. "Especially to dear old friends like yourself, for I am only a working girl. Don't you need any decorating in your new apartment?"

"That depends," said Batty. "If we can staht the ball rolling in Harlem again—if friend Buster would cooperate, we might all do something and make something again."

"Cooperate how?" said irritated Buster. "You're going to shoot that crap again?"

"It's no crap, fellah. You've got a whale on the bat if you'd only go to it. I've been telling him, Patsinette, that he is the one person can bring white folks with money back to Harlem, like it used to be in Millinda's time. And this is the beginning right here."

"This is *indeed* a nice party," said Patsinette. "The liquor is excellent and the people are nice."

"It only needs a few high-class whites," said Batty, "them that wants the best stuff in Harlem and can pay for it. I knew you would finally come right back to my street," he added, to Buster. "Now that Charlotte is backing you, we will all help."

"What d'you mean, backing me?" said Buster. "Backing me to do what?"

"Stop kidding, sweet-back, *you* know what I mean. Can't I see you're on easy street again, you hot dog. I suggested the way but I couldsn't start you. Only a woman can help a man like that. Cohse, Charlotte ain't got Millinda's money, but you can make a lot outa your experience, once you get the start."

"Charlotte is not interested in me the way you think she is," said Buster.

"Oh, jest listen to the lamb, Patsinette. Why, man, every time that woman looks at you I sees love shining in her eyes."

"She's got a husband if you don't know it, and please quite talking about Charlotte that way," Buster spoke in a low hard tone.

Batty chuckled: "Now get off that dime. You know a husband in Harlem don't phase no cullud woman. Millinda had a husband, when you were sweet, didn't she? And he wasn't paralyzed, neither."

Batty dug his thumb into Buster's ribs and, winking at Patsinette, said: "Good ol' Buster, you're all right. A good man may fall down, but you can't keep him down when he's got that getting-up stuff like you got."

Suddenly enraged against Batty, Buster savagely swung his fist into his mouth, saying: "Keep your stinking mouth offa Charlotte, you plug-ugly mugger-fugger." Batty fell crashing against the radio into the couch, smashing a lamp and breaking glasses. Tillie Ashmead jumped up screaming as if she had been hit, but it was only a glass of liquor spilled into the lap of her party frock. Charlotte rushed up to Buster and with both hands seized the lapels of his coat. "Why did you do it, Buster? What made you spoil the pahty?"

"Because the damned hog of a nigger started talking dirt about you after drinking up your liquor. I'm sick o' them anyhow. I tell you they are all no damned good."

Buster strode from the room. Outside the keen autumn air brought him down from his high excitement, and he felt a little regretful of his act. "I should have thought of the guests, too. Charlotte invited them. And after all, everything was for me. Yet, I spoiled the party. I'm a self-destroyer."

Up and down through Harlem, keeping to the side streets, he marched for hours, brooding, murmuring, alone. Tired at last, he entered a colored cafe on Seventh Avenue. As he walked in he noticed Baldwin Hatcher drinking at the bar. He was about to make a quick retreat, but Hatcher called to him. Buster joined Hatcher at the end of the bar and attempted to apologize.

Hatcher checked him: "No need to apologize to me. What you did was all right so far as I was concerned. I understand." He ordered Scotch whisky for both.

"All the same I feel like hell, messing up everything like that," said Buster. "But I couldn't stand that hawg. He stinks in Harlem."

"Forget him, then," said Hatcher. "Drink up and let's talk about something else."

Baldwin Hatcher was a former journalist, who had been famous in the glamor days of Millinda's ascendancy. His syndicated column, "The Big Town," was read by millions. His style was intimate, like conversation, and most popular. Many writers, imagining it was easy, attempted to emulate him. But none ever penetrated his secret of processing his simple-appearing word pictures. He was as inimitable as Charlie Chaplin and when he stopped writing, his place was never filled.

Hatcher had invented a palatable potpourri of the big and little marvels of New York. He mingled the rich and comfortable and the poor and miserable together in one column with enjoyment to all. Famous and exclusive places and exotic and obscure places were all beautiful to look at in his column, which to millions was the guide to New York. Perhaps no other journalist could have accomplished the feat of placing on the society page of a great newspaper the picture of Millinda, hostess of Harlem, illustrated by a decorous feature article. But Baldwin Hatcher did it, and millions of whites delighted in it.

Baldwin Hatcher was sitting grandly on the top of his world when a revolution shook the world of big business. The wonder pile of his great newspaper crashed and he was hurled down. He never got up in that sphere again. He was handicapped by the bigness he had attained. He became one of the unemployed. Former colleagues avoided him. Younger emulators who had hailed him as master now discerned flaws in the thing they had called his "superb technique." They began to discover that it had been rather "antique."

For some years Baldwin Hatcher remained like one forgotten by the public. Until America was startled by his radio voice. It was discovered that his voice was splendidly radiophonetic. He developed a radio feature, popular yet distinguished. The public adored it, even more than his column. Fan letters attested to the popularity of the Hatcher Radio Hour. Big advertisers beseeched Hatcher, offering huge sums, merely to be mentioned. As he limited himself to a few and was fastidious about the firms he advertised, he had a large waiting list. His income was vastly superior to what he had received as a columnist. And many of the colleagues who had ignored him sought him out now to seek favors.

Hatcher rarely made an appearance in Harlem as he had often done in the wild Prohibition era. When he was in eclipse, he sometimes visited quietly one of the less popular speakeasies. Charlotte was the only Harlemite with whom he was still very friendly. Besides Millinda, perhaps she was the only person he had really liked. Moreover, the social milieu of the Harlem that he knew no longer existed. If he could not like Buster, warmly and humanly as he liked Charlotte, he nevertheless admired him as a type.

Buster told Hatcher he felt that everybody and everything in Harlem were against him. It was as if there were a conspiracy against him. The old crowd was mocking at him. He felt it in their attitude, even though they were not all as offensive as Batty. "I guess they resented me all the time because I was Millinda's friend. And now I am out of luck they have a chance to show it. We Negroes are a lot of crabs in a barrel, pulling down anyone what's trying to climb out."

"It's the same among my folks," said Hatcher. "You know them only as benevolent employers or as friendly guests visiting Harlem. But my folks are crabs in the barrel and dogs in the manger just like your folks. I experienced almost exactly what you are passing through now. It was a little different, of course. But when I got out of journalism, I was cold-shouldered by some of my best friends. Behind my back they said I was finished. Now I've made a comeback in radio, they all come fawning like dogs. They want a thousand things: radio publicity for friends and charitable affairs with which they are connected for their own social advancement."

"You had a marvelous comeback, but it's because the white folks' crab-barrel is bigger than the colored folks' own," said Buster. "I am partly right. When a white man falls it's easier for him to rise again than a colored man, for he has more room to scramble. You know that."

Hatcher agreed. "Yet there is still a lot of room in your group, if your people would realize it and exploit it. But you let *my* folks do it instead. Who is really reaping the profits off of Harlem's dancing and singing and drinking and eating but my people—white people?''

"You're right about that, I guess,'' said Buster.

"Of course I am,'' said Baldwin Hatcher. "For example, I played a big joke when I put Millinda all over the society page of a New York newspaper, but it wasn't a joke on your people, for it helped put Harlem on the map as a special quarter, like Chinatown. Harlem attracted tourists and slummers. If your influential Harlemites were wise and alert, they would have started establishments for that new trade. But they let the gangsters of my tribe hog it.''

"All the same you can't make a Chinatown out of Harlem,'' said Buster. "Niggers are the native Americans.''

"And that's just why they should make the Negrotowns better than the Chinatowns all over America,'' said Hatcher. "I'd rather see colored people exploiting and building up themselves than a gang of white gangsters taking it all. I know what I am talking about, Buster, for I was born South like you. Only I was educated up here. Let's have another drink.''

"I guess this race business is a big racket,'' said Buster, swallowing his Scotch.

"Sure, like the whole business of life everywhere,'' said Hatcher.

Buster bowed his head to the bar momentarily as if trying to recollect something. Then he said: "Guess it would be good if I could get out of Harlem again for a change. But I don't know where to go. Maybe one of those camps would do me some good.''

"I could give you some money or a loan, if you prefer,'' said Hatcher, "but that won't solve your problem.''

"I know it. I think I would really like to go to one of those camps. I've been everything but a soldier and I won't have to enlist,'' Buster laughed.

"If you are serious, I could introduce you to a big man in that set-up, who might fix something for you,'' said Hatcher.

"I *am* serious and I'll be glad if you can put me in touch with this person,'' said Buster.

"All right, I'll give you a letter to him. Can you come down to my office tomorrow afternoon? About three?''

"Sure I can.''

Hatcher gave Buster his card.

8
NEWFIELDS

So Buster went to Camp Newfields. Newfields was one of the havens of the new era. There a number of unemployed working men from the city were sent for rehabilitation. Most of them had voluntarily left relief rolls, preferring to work on a relief farm for the same amount that would have been doled out to them in the city. The men as a whole were too old for the Civilian Conservation Camps, although there were some youngsters among them.

The fine property was set in a fertile country, sixty-five miles northward of Manhattan. There were three hundred and fifty acres of land. It comprised a massive main building for the men, an annex where new men were temporarily lodged, a three-story house for the director, a cottage for an assistant director, a large garage, a carpenter's shop, and a vast barn. Formerly it was a reformatory. When it was taken over as an experimental farm for unemployed men, it was renamed Newfields.

The place was expected to accommodate 1000 men. The main building was equipped to house 650, the barracks-like annex about 250. It was considered a self-governing institution. The director and his assistant did the planning. The supervisors of the departments worked out the plans with the men. Out on the farm the men plowed and planted potatoes, corn, beans, carrots and other vegetables. But the bulk of the food consumed came from the city.

The men were selected from a list of city workers. The ordinary wage paid was $5.50 fortnightly, the same amount as was allotted to a single man on relief in the city. One-half of this amount was deducted for maintenance. And out of the balance the men had to purchase clothing, which they paid for on the installment plan. Nearly all of them required special boots and clothes for the farm.

The majority of the men were Irish. The rest were of old Yankee stock, Scandinavians, Italians, Poles, Aframericans and others. The working day began after breakfast, which lasted from 7 until 9, and ended at 4. All the men ate together in the immense dining room.

The director was formerly a scoutmaster. The men called him "colonel." His assistant was a Tammany politician. The supervisors of the departments were drawn from all the different groups: Irish, Italian, Jewish, German, etc.—all, excepting the Aframerican.

When Buster arrived at Newfields, he was assigned to the recreation department, as a kind of special assistant. He pounded swing tunes out of the piano, gave exhibitions of the Lindy Hop and suchlike dances, organized a sing-song of colored and white members, and helped design costumes and scenery. There were forty-five colored men at Newfields. They had their own clan like the Irish and also the Italians, although there was a general spirit of camaraderie among all of the men.

In the evening those who did not trail off to the villages gathered in the recreation room to play cards, checkers, dominoes, picture puzzles, or read or write letters. Some who preferred music went to the music room to practice. Moving pictures were shown once a week. And sometimes a group of actors arrived from the city to put on a special performance.

The routine work of the place was competently done. The buildings, furniture, walls, floors and baths were kept in excellent condition. The "colonel" continually boasted that he was getting high-class work done at a low cost, which would confound the economists. His attitude to the men, whom he called "my boys" or "my gang," was paternal, with a mixture of naive patronage. The men were not generally contented with their status. There was plenty of food, but little variety. The leisure-time was adequate and relieved by games, yet everybody suffered from an indefinable ennui. The men were the best of a lot of skilled and unskilled unemployed. The percentage of white-collar workers—mainly store and office clerks—was high, and deliberately kept down. All the men dreaded a return to the old ways in the city, yet they saw no hope, no solution of their problem in Newfields.

The men reacted against the attitude of the country residents, who were generally resentful of the invasion from the city. The local residents referred to the men as bums. Some of them had blundered when the place was first opened. They made the mistake of selling their labor to the neighboring farmers during their leisure time and over the weekend picking apples, strawberries, and making hay, etc., for much less than the average pay. Skilled men worked in the villages for almost nothing. In one amazing case an Italian saloonkeeper had had a fine garage built for a song. All that the workmen received in payment was booze. They had figured upon obtaining free booze for a long time after that garage was completed. But when it was finished, the saloonkeeper informed them that they had drunk up during the construction all the booze that the garage was worth! The country people were shocked by these men from the big city, where organized labor was so powerful, selling themselves so cheap.

Yet Newfields itself proved eloquently that the men were not just a lot of bums. In a few weeks the place had been transformed into a model farm. Important officials and visitors went there to see and praise the work. The "colonel" was kept busy showing the achievement to visitors. Yet proud though he was of the achievement, he had little sympathy for the social and political momentum which had made Newfields possible. He was a New Deal official who did not believe in the New Deal, but the intricate play of politics had carried him along on a progressive tide and made of a reactionary an unconvinced New Dealer. He really thought that the power of the New Deal was founded upon the popular resentment of a thirsty nation, and once he said that its symbol should be a foaming stein of beer.

The regulation against boozing was stringent. Any man discovered drunk in any form was sent away from Newfields. In lecturing to the men the "colonel" often said that the majority of the men in the unemployable class were there because of booze.

The men were allowed to submit suggestions and plans to improve the running of the place. Also they were allowed to think they could be critical. But the men as a body did not exercise the privilege. For, everywhere, there were informers who reported to the director what the men were thinking. There were rumors of "reds" on the farm, although none of the men seemed to know any. But often the "colonel" would mount a table after dinner or supper and harangue the men on Americanism. He said that he had heard of things said about Newfields that could only be said by "reds," but he believed that the majority of the men believed in Americanism and would not be misled by "reds." He said that every man had the right to make complaint directly to him, but he would not tolerate any agitation.

From the common ennui some of the men craved surcease in booze. But few had enough money to buy even the cheapest stuff. To gratify the craving a number of them took to drinking rubbing alcohol. Some became half crazed from the poisonous stuff and were sent away down to Bellevue.

One Saturday a truck driver named Larry went wild. He was born in the city of New York and lived there all of his 39 years. He was a likeable fellow and friendly with everybody. That fatal Saturday all the capital he possessed was nine cents. He and a few friends went to the village. They hadn't enough money to obtain beer and so they pooled their nickels to buy rubbing alcohol.

The poison touched Larry's brain and started him off on mad gyrations. He went swinging his fists right and left through the main street. Scared, the villagers deserted the street. Some of his pals who remained sane tried to hold down Larry. He knocked them out. He jumped on the seat of a wagon, chased the driver off and tore down the street as if the devil were roasting his and the horse's tail. When he stopped, he pulled his shirt off and began beating up his chest. Finally he dived crashing straight through the plate glass of the largest grocery store and was sliced as if he had been shaved by a cutting machine. An ugly, bloody business, he was conveyed back to Newfields, given first aid by the doctor there and sent off to Bellevue.

The debacle of Larry set all the men agog. Something was wrong, they reasoned, that such a fine fellow should have met such a fate. But although the men felt sorry for Larry, everybody was careful of his words. The brainiest men worked in the offices and were the most careful of all, for a few of their number, for talking too much, had been put to do the work of the brawniest. Men in the offices who came into disfavor with the management were punished by being sent to work on the farm. Skilled workmen who had boldly gone through strikes and picketing were humbled and afraid at Newfields. They had all felt that even working for nothing in the backwoods was better than idleness on relief in the city.

However, William, one of Larry's pals, who was in charge of the stables, forthrightly expressed his dissatisfaction with the way of things. William was a teetotaler, a lanky fellow who always illustrated conversation with jokes. He possessed the primitive ingredients of leadership, and a group of men could always be found around him. So William talked to some of his listeners about Larry and doing something to change things a little in Newfields. He said that instead of making individual suggestions or complaints to the "colonel," the men should have the right to get together in a body and elect a committee to represent them.

William received a good response from the men to whom he mentioned his idea. These men got in touch with others and soon there was a group of them all thinking along the same lines. A meeting was arranged. At the same time there was a whispering among the men that they were being swindled by somebody. Out of the fortnightly pittance of $5.50, they were paying for clothing that was really intended to be issued free to them. Some men said that in the city they got the same kind of clothing free. The whispering grew long and big until every man of the rank and file became aware.

William decided to hold a secret meeting with a number of the more reliable men.

Buster was popular with the men in the recreation room. They applauded his amateur stage work and rated him a good fellow. One of William's confidantes apprised Buster of the meeting. Buster was as ignorant as a buck about the New Deal and labor. But in his gypsy soul there was a sense of human justice. Newfields for him was a makeshift for hard times, and no paradise.

Buster confided in Opal, his buddy who worked in the laundry. They both shared the same room and that day when Buster heard that the men were being skinned of their miserable pittance, he and Opal stayed up half the night whispering about it. Even to Buster, who had lived the best of his existence in the parasitic world, such a mean way of parasitism was horrible, unbelievable. They agreed to wait until the meeting was held and then acquaint some of the other colored men of the decisions.

The meeting was held one Saturday after dinner. The men had wandered off singly and in pairs so as not to excite suspicion. It was a good time for the meeting, for on a Saturday afternoon some of the men played games and others wandered off to roam the woods. William's group met by a stream in a clearing hidden by trees. It was autumn and the grass was grey-green and crisp. There were about 50 men. They squatted about and William in the midst began talking.

First he spoke of Larry as a representative type of all workers who dreaded demoralization in the city and had chosen coming to Newfields hoping there to keep up their morale as men. The place looked like a success, William declared. It appeared to be running smoothly on the surface, but every week they were sending away a few of the best men, men like Larry. And they were leaving worse off than when they came. Who knew how many of them had been hurried away to the city to die?

William was a good speaker to stir up the emotions: "I am a teetotaler," he said, "and always have been. But most of my best friends drink liquor. I'd like to know why up here in God's good country men have to take rubbing alcohol as a substitute for the real drink. If they had just a little more pocket change, they would not want to drink poison." Then William started in telling about the clothing swindle, which all the men were eager to hear about. The rumor, he heard, was started by a confidential clerk, who had been sent away for drunkenness. But it appeared that there was a lot of truth in that rumor. They were paying for clothing which was specially sent up to be distributed free to the men on the farm. They were being robbed of tobacco money.

When William finished, a general discussion started. William directed it and tried to answer the questions. The men argued that there were no chronic drunkards among them. The craving for alcoholic drinks was a natural one, and the men drank rubbing alcohol because it was the only thing they could afford to buy. Paying for food and clothes left them without any pocket money. And there was that rumor that they were being swindled of pocket money. The men grew excited as they discussed it. Some said it might have been better to remain in the city on relief than to stay in the country working like slaves and then getting skinned and going crazy.

"Talking only won't do any good," one fellow said excitedly. "Let's march on the office in a body and talk straight to the 'colonel.'"

"That's a good idea," others agreed.

William was cautioning them to wait and carefully plan out something, when the "colonel" broke through the clearing and started rapidly talking. "You agitators and traitors! I heard that you were plotting to disrupt our institution, planning a riot, kidnap the officials and run things yourself. Well gang, you can start right now or never. You hear me! If you have bombs and machine guns, use them on me! Start at once! One! Two! Three!"

The "colonel" held up his hands. "I am not afraid. I have come here alone to face you all because I am not afraid—not afraid," he barked in a strangely fearful pitch. "I have treated you men squarely. There is a standing rule that any man can come straight to me with a complaint. Yet you have sneaked off to organize against ME.

"I knew that there were Communists in Newfields. The Communists go everywhere creating trouble. Communist agitators are paid $5 a day. Are you men allowing yourselves to be fooled? You men chose to come up here because you were in need. Will you allow Communists to stir up trouble among you? You are Americans, aren't you? You believe in Americanism, don't you?"

"Yeah," some of the men said.

"Then stop your secret meetings and discussions and come straight out in the open like real American men. If any one of you finds anything wrong, bring your complaint directly to me. I am an American and must treat you like one. There is an American way of doing things. And now, gang, it's up to you to disperse peacefully."

The meeting broke up; the men scattered in twos and threes, discussing the issues and most of them in favor of the "colonel." Someone had informed on the meeting and the "colonel" had chosen the psychological moment to act. The majority of the men admired the way he had surprised and plainly talked to them. They were divided about the swindle. Instead of seeing it as an administrative issue, many were inclined to take it as a personal thing and said that they felt more like men buying their own clothing, even if they never had pocket money, than to accept a free gift of it.

That evening and the following day an interesting bit of information was carefully circulated among the men, stating that the "colonel" and the staff were making strenuous efforts to put Newfields on a self-supporting basis with the possibility of making it a model for the nation.

The information purported to come from an authoritative source, although it was not an official circular typed and signed by the director or his assistant, as was the usual custom. But the body of the men reacted favorably to it. They felt proud of being the pioneers of a great experiment. They had fled the city because they were ashamed of the stigma of idleness and accepting relief grants. They were willing to make any sacrifice to prove that work relief was a national asset.

The following afternoon Buster was in an anteroom of the recreation hall looking over some old masks and costumes to stage a show when the "colonel" entered.

Said he: "That *was* a surprise to find you with that gang of troublemakers. I didn't expect a colored man to be disloyal and unpatriotic. You know, of course, that when you came here you were specially recommended to me. I talked to you personally and found a congenial place for you. That is something I rarely do—even for *white* men. Perhaps you don't know that there are Southerners on this lot who have kicked about colored and white men mixing together and eating in the same dining room. I told them I was a Northerner and believed in equal treatment for all Americans and that if they did not like the way Newfields was run, they could get to hell back to the city. My administration would not tolerate any discrimination. Yet you, the most intelligent colored man up here, are holding in with a gang that don't mean your kind any good."

"It was just the right and proper thing for you not to tolerate discrimination, Colonel, for discrimination is un-American and unconstitutional," said Buster.

"Since you seem to know a lot about what is un-American and unconstitutional, you should also know better than siding with Communist agitators."

"Those men weren't Communists, Colonel. I haven't heard any man talk Communism since I've been up here."

"The Communists are cleverer than you think, and know how to conceal their identity," said the "colonel."

The following day William and eleven other men were transferred to work relief units on Staten Island and Long Island. William and two others refused the transfer and left for the city. A number of the men were taken off inside work and sent out on the farm. Opal was removed from the laundry and put on the plough. Buster was sent to the kitchen to peel potatoes and scrub pots.

Buster and Opal agreed to quit at once. "I've got enough," said Buster. "If I stay on, this place will sure get me like Larry and land me in the psycho ward at Bellevue."

"I leave mah woman working part time and come up here," said Opal. "I was fed up with hogs' ends and loving all the time. She cried and begged me not to leave, but I felt like I was becoming like a cheap sissified sweet-back. And brother that morning I was leaving she shook her breast at me and says, 'You kain't live without it, honey, you gotta come back soon to mamma.' I aint nevah regret leaving for Newfields done rejobinated me. But I wouldn't stand for no boss kicking me around and telling me I kain't get together to talk with mah pals."

"I'm foot-free and heart-loose of the female problem right now," said Buster. But if William and those fellows were Communists, then President Roosevelt and his cabinet must be Communists, too. Well, we've been up here over three months. Maybe the sidewalks won't be so hard on our feet now."

9
TWO LEADERS

Buster left Newfields for New York with a new determination. At least Newfields had helped him emerge from his state of confusion. His head was better, his eyes keener to appreciate Harlem and gauge the tempo of the movement of the big colored center.

Buster went directly to look up Charlotte Poynter. But robust Charlotte had died, leaving her frail paralytic husband. Buster discovered Mr. Poynter in the care of some cultists known as the Glory Soulers. To his amazement he found that Oleander Powers, the young college girl who had lodged with Charlotte, was also a member of the cult. It was she who had persuaded Mr. Poynter to join.

Oleander was not the only educated colored girl captivated by cultism. There were many more in Harlem: college and high school girls who had been lured into one form of cultism because of the magic appeal, the glamor, the comfortable living it offered in a Harlem swamped by Depression. Colored college men also were joining the cults in astonishing numbers. But mainly they were the older men—bankrupt lawyers, doctors, realtors.

If the numbers game is the greatest industrial phenomenom in Harlem, cultism is the greatest spiritual phenomenom. Colored Harlem within its thickly populated area is honeycombed with cults. Yet the pure forms of Christianity, Catholic and Protestant, are flourishing, prosperous in grand temples. Harlem lays claim to the largest church in America and in the world.

Watching the large Sunday crowds pouring out of the legitimate churches one would imagine there were no people left for membership in the strange cults founded upon a marriage of primitive Christian mysticism and African black magic and fetishism. But another person attending any of the overcrowded meetings of the cults would imagine that all the people of Harlem were cultists. However, many of the regular churchgoers were also frequenters of the semi-secret spiritualist chapels, which had stimulated a formidable growth of esoterism in Harlem.

The great religions—Islamism, Hinduism, Buddhism and Judaism—were interpreted as occult sciences in private apartments, which were furbished to represent Indian temples, Egyptian pyramids, Juda-Ethiopian arks and Moorish mosques. Crescents, lotus flowers, palm fronds, miniature Cleopatra's needles were used as symbols. Some of the male spiritualists were actually East Indians and Egyptians and Arabians. They were married to American colored women, cultists who had inducted them into exploiting their foreign language and appearance in the mystic business. Out of the combination they reaped little fortunes.

Mainly the spiritualists received and delivered messages from dead relatives, foretold the future and guessed the lucky numbers. All this was accompanied by an elaborate esoteric ritual, litanies in jargon and strange languages and the burning of colored candles and incense. Negroes who followed the crude rites of Obeahism, Voodooism and Conjurism in the West Indies and in the southern states discovered their particular fetish refined in the spiritualist chapels. As white gangsters had organized the numbers racket and eliminated the many "hits," Harlem by thousands resorted to the spiritualists to get the divination of the lucky number. And the lucky number candles of all colors were burning in Harlem. Fat little five cent candles were sold by the spiritualists for 25 cents, 50 cents, and sometimes $1, according to the way of the spirit's working and the previous appraisal of a client's renumerative resources.

BLUE CANDLES burning for joy, peace and fortune.
RED CANDLES burning for love, bringing love, increasing love.
BLACK CANDLES burning away evil and enemies.
GREEN CANDLES burning for good business and success against rivalry.
PURPLE CANDLES burning for domination over all things, for self-mastery, influence, power.
YELLOW CANDLES burning for the true religion.
ORANGE CANDLES burning for lucky dreams.
BROWN CANDLES burning for secret things.
WHITE CANDLES burning for sweet communion with the dead.
PINK CANDLES burning for GOOD LUCK and SUCCESS.

With their secret and esoteric rites the spiritualist chapels were not a challenge to the regular churches as open cults. Of the many cults in Harlem the Glory Soulers attracted the greatest attention and received the largest publicity. The head of the cult was called the Glory Savior. He was a full-sized, light-complexioned man. His followers were known as Glory Souls. Ridiculed at first, especially by the colored press, the Glory Soulers were quickly recognized as a serious cult when they were noticed by the white press and thereby achieved national publicity.

The Glory Savior was no ordinary ignorant Negro preacher. Formerly he was Robert Byrd and once operated an employment agency in Harlem. In this venture he had a partner named Luther Sharpage. For five years prior to 1929, the agency was one of the most successful in Harlem. But in the beginning of the nineteen thirties private employment agencies in Harlem, receiving no calls for work, were so beseiged by thousands of out-of-work that most of them closed up. Perhaps the first American sit-down really occurred in Harlem when an employment agent, unable to pay rent and utilities bills, walked out of his place, leaving it to a crowd of job-seekers. They camped there for weeks (many had no place to sleep), foddering collectively by all the available means, until the landlord finally evicted them.

It might have been that incident that supplied Byrd and Sharpage with the idea of The Helping Hand. The partners rented and furnished an old tenement building in Fifth Avenue. They ran it on a cheap cooperative plan. For those for whom they found employment they provided cheap lodging. Four and even six persons were put in one room, two in one bed. A common kitchen was established, food bought at bargain rates and all ate together. Byrd and Sharpage and their wives joined in the common meal.

Most of the Helping Handers were women. As good domestic jobs were difficult to find, the women usually went out hunting for day's work. The housewives of the Bronx employ a large percentage of Harlem's cheap domestic labor, and so the colored women used to gravitate to certain points in the Bronx and wait there for white matrons to come and hire them. The patronage swelled to such large proportions that in later years the main point of congregation became notorious as the Bronx Slave Market. Such workers were quick and glad to accept whatever wages were offered, and they got little indeed. Many had been forced out of their apartments, could not even afford a small single room and liked the clean, if crowded, atmosphere of the Helping Hand home. Leaving work, they did not need to go home to do their own cleaning up, which was one of the ordeals of the domestic workers of Harlem. Under the collective system of The Helping Hand those members who were unemployed did the work of the hostel while the employed were at work.

Byrd and Sharpage sent out cards to comfortable and wealthy families all over New York, soliciting jobs in the name of The Helping Hand. They guaranteed efficiency, honesty, sobriety and regularity in their workers. The Helping Hand job scheme worked so beautifully that within the year of its start, another house was opened. The members established a custom of getting together to pray and sing morning and evening. Observing the enthusiasm and joyous fraternal spirit of these meetings, Byrd decided to join in with them. Byrd might have been a great dramatic actor had he been born into a different world, as he was so quick to perceive and enter into all the emotions of people. Praying and singing with his people he soon discovered in himself a persuasive preacher and that he had power over women especially and could excite them to shouting and swaying.

Noticing that those who were most fervent in praying and singing were the most enthusiastic workers, he conceived the idea of harnessing religion to his Helping Hand plan of work. Upon this issue Sharpage disagreed with Byrd. Sharpage was more intellectual than Byrd. He contended that there were too many churches and cults in Harlem and it would be better if colored folk were not so possessed with religion.

At first the difference between the two men was not sharp. Sharpage confined himself to the routine work of keeping up the establishment, ordering supplies and supervising account books. But in the interval his wife died, and the female Byrd espoused his point of view. She had been inclined to it for some time and had expressed the opinion that the male Byrd was spending too much energy singing with the women. With the woman between them, the jealousy of Byrd made the difference sharper and finally came the open split. The partnership was dissolved, Sharpage holding one of the houses, but Mrs. Byrd quit her mate to go with him.

Mrs. Byrd's defection unloosened the remaining women's emotions, and Robert Byrd was overwhelmed with their sympathy. At the meetings they sang and swayed and shouted again and again their faith in him and his work. They called him savior. Other people were attracted. The movement grew into a cult, with Robert Byrd preaching a new salvation for souls. Soon he became known as Glory Savior and his following as Glory Souls. That following came largely from the lowest-down strata of the colored masses. Hundreds were drawn from the churches.

The movement spread with rapturous noise and eclat. There were special reasons for its magnetic appeal. The Glory Savior's new society was based on certain laws such as: non-sex, non-mortality, non-race, non-color, collective work, collective living, collective recreation and complete faith in him as savior. Every member was obliged to add ''Glory'' to his name. As the Glory Soulers gave up all for the Savior, more properties were acquired by the cult. And the business of the souls became one of the important items of Harlem's economy. Cars were purchased for the more glorified dignitaries, buses for the rank and file, pianos and equipment for dining halls and kitchens. A large staff of secretaries, stenographers, typists and clerks was maintained.

But the thing that brought national and international fame to the Glory Soulers was the amazing white miracle. Cryptically Glory Savior had announced to his followers that he was fasting, passing through a period of special gestation in anticipation of a marvel of a miracle. It was, he emphasized, a white miracle. The oracle omnipotent had stirred him and he had seen the vision. The fasting alone was extraordinary, for although the Glory Soulers had renounced carnal life, they largely indulged in the sensual delights of eating and drinking and dancing and laughing, which were their outstanding virtues. The miracle happened one afternoon in the major Glory Home. In the midst of black and brown arms extended like naked branches of trees swaying in the wind and saluting the Savior, wonderful stomping feet and voices mellow like molasses in sweet praise, an expansive white, white-haired matriarch marched up the aisle, the dancing souls clearing an avenue for the apparition, and took her stand beside Glory Savior. Despite her considerable age and the portliness of her figure, there was decided grace in her regal movement. And the Glory Soulers were more reckless in their dancing in anticipation of her testimony. Uplifting his hand for silence, which instantly prevailed, Glory Savior announced: "I Glory Savior do radiotelephotograph to you, my souls, the transformation of the glorification of the miracle for which you have been watching and waiting. Without doctrine and without creed, without class, without race, without color, I bring you the gift of souls: universally men and women are made one without difference united in the unity of all souls. Welcome souls another Glory Soul."

Like thunder claps shouted greetings filled the building: "Glory! Glory to all souls! Glory to the Savior! Glory to the new soul! Glory to the highest!"

The portentous person lifted up her hands and said: "Glory Savior! Glory all souls with whom I am glorified and freed from the domination of the body. I was surfeited with the life of the world, inflated with pomp and flattery and rich feeding, living in grand style, visiting and receiving visits from others like myself, occupied with dictating to servants and worries by relations. Oh the fussiness of living in the flesh!

"I longed for release and salvation. But I was like a person living in a magnificent gilded prison, equipped with all modern conveniences. Indeed, friendly souls, my nice house was a prison. I knew it and that I had to be released from it. But I knew I could not be released by my people. But I dreamed of a savior, a savior among another people. And soon after my dream I heard about our Glory Savior, and I knew he was the answer to my dreaming.

"So I prepared to leave the prison and go to the savior's home. And as soon as I made the great decision my life was different. For my savior also knew and was helping me. I had no need of servants to help nor relations to advise me about my grand journey. Everything was prepared like a miracle. And when I was ready to go, I discovered a robe all covered with money. It is here for all to see." Two little brown girl souls at the back of the platform came forward with a robe and slipped it on the great new soul. It was fabric of shining silver and laden with bills of large denominations.

"It was the price of my release from prison. Oh look at me, fellow souls! I may be bulky in your eyes, but I am truly transformed. Oh I feel as small as a lamb and as light as a bird and, glory to the savior, I can leap and dance like a free soul with you."

The new soul broke into a swinging stomping, her vast frame heaving and quivering like a gigantic figure of rubber set atop a float and dominating a glorious carnival. "Glory Savior! Glory new soul! Glory to all glory souls!" A mighty chorus of shouting uplifted the congregation, and, the band swinging the Glory Hymn, all the people began swaying, dancing closely, warmly together.

The newcomer was given the name of Glory Queen Mother and although color did not exist in the cult, it was doubtless because she was white and reputedly wealthy that she was accorded such a highly glorified place. The savior's new wife held the title of Glory Queen. The Glory Soulers seemingly did not know or care where the new soul came from and what strata of white society she had deserted to join the cult. But the fact that she had joined the cult was released and became a news item of national importance.

Meanwhile, Glory Savior's former partner had not remained inactive. Luther Sharpage also had something of the quality of mystery about him. It was presumed that he had been in service during the World War, probably as a sailor, and that he had remained abroad and traveled extensively. No one knew exactly how, but he knew a lot about Europe and the East. It was practical first-hand knowledge. He knew a smattering of many languages. Sharpage liked to boast that he was an international student.

Harlem strangely was the haven of many suchlike characters. Dark people from various parts of the world, coming to New York, had gravitated there after finding socially uncongenial living in other sections. There were dark complexioned East Indians (Hindus and Moslems), Arabs, Puerto Ricans and other Latin Americans, Africans from the North, the West, the East and the South, besides a large colony of West Indians. A goodly number of these foreign colored people posed as native Americans, because of a certain antagonism existing between the native-born colored people and the foreign. Others preferred not to reveal their identity, according to the special racket in which they were interested. The origin of many of its residents is one of the perennial interesting topics of conversation in Harlem. Even the native-born Aframericans give a lot of their leisure time to discussion of the quality of the white mixed with their black blood and some who could afford it were paying well for the tracing of their family trees.

Now after a period of eclipse, Sharpage appeared on the streets of Harlem wearing a turban, a belted leather coat, boots and spurs and announcing himself as Omar, The African, founder of a new religion and a new idea of labor for the colored masses. The new religion was a philosophical form of Islam as it had been evolved in Africa, said Omar, and the new conception of labor for the colored masses was to be worked out in the Yeomen of Labor, which he had organized.

Haranguing Harlem from a stepladder on the street corners, Omar, more than any other soapboxer, drew the crowds. Young men, high-school lads among them, stopped to listen and decided to follow him. The colored man was naturally religious, said Omar. But it was necessary for him to have a new religion. A religion suited to Negro needs. The new phenomenom in the social world was the rise of labor and the power of the worker. The white world was shedding its old skin of Capitalism to take on the new skin of Labor. But it was changing its religion to adapt itself to the transformation. Only colored people were clinging to the old religion. Colored people were notoriously a working people, traditionally hewers of wood and drawers of water, according to the old religion. Let us wake up and transform ourselves to find ourselves in the new world of the earth and not of the Glory Sky.

During the hot summer and in the balmy fall Omar in the evening rhetorically preached his new idea. During the day he worked hard and practically with his followers at the organization of the Yeomen of Labor. His new idea embodied the closer unity of all colored people as a group and the intensive reconstruction of the colored community. He drew up a program for the community. Omar's plan had features of local autonomy. He charted the colored community, showing that the majority of the residents were domestic servants, all working outside of the community. He showed that high school and college graduates were mainly engaged in domestic work, excepting the fortunate few who became social workers. He demanded that the white employers established in the colored community and exploiting residents should not employ white clerks only but also colored clerks. He demanded that the larger percentage of municipal employees of the higher and lower ranks in the community should be colored, so that instead of always appearing abnormal like a foreign section run by outsiders, the colored community would gradually take on the aspect of other American communities.

The movement of Omar and the cult of the Glory Soul had divided Harlem's common people into two camps. While the great mass of plain people, following the tradition of old time religion, was partial to Glory Soul, many of the young vanguard of workers who were caught in the toils of Depression were inclined to listen to Omar. The conservative colored leaders and the intelligentsia, while scoffing at Glory Soul and inclined to take his cult humorously in spite of its increasing numbers, were openly skeptical of and even hostile to Omar. And it was significant that while the large following of Glory Soul was mainly women who had long lost their youth, Omar's followers were all young men and women.

Powerfully built and possessing a deep compelling voice, Omar thundered from the corner of Seventh Avenue: "We colored folks need glorious bodies and not glorious souls. This is the age of the New Deal and a new society is forming. We got to get in on the ground floor now. The New Deal is building up depressed communities. Are we going to keep on hoping and waiting like Uncle Tom in the white folks' backyard or get up and get in on the New Deal to build up our colored communities on the other side of the tracks?

"That is the question I am asking in Harlem. Where are the colored leaders leading the colored people? That is the question you people must ask. You got to bellow it loud and long until the leaders they get scared. Worry them to death until they give you the answer.

"The big noise in Harlem today is the Glory Savior and Glory Souls. While the white folks are marching along the New Deal line, this Glory Savior is snaring the colored people with a New Dope. No more colored bodies, only souls living in Glory Homes. No more fighting for our rights, for Glory Savior protects us. Three hundred years out of the African jungle, yet the medicine man is still in our midst ruling us with his fetish. Three hundred years and we're still following the maker of magic.''

There was no stratum of Harlem society which Omar's voice did not reach directly or indirectly. For the highest and lowest of Harlem's thousands passed there where he spoke on the corner of Seventh Avenue. Preachers, teachers and students, doctors, lawyers and business men, welfare officials, welfare workers, nurses, politicians, artists, writers, numbers kings and queens, big-time procurers, courtesans white and colored all mingled together promenading along the boulevard and animating the scene like a Spanish plaza. Many lingered awhile with the crowd to listen to Omar.

The audience that listened to Glory Soul was not so representative, for Glory Soul never spoke in the street. When any of the skeptical intelligentsia went to hear him in his Glory Home, they went mostly in a group, similar to a theater party. Yet the two movements of Glory Soul and of Omar respectively were like a two-faced mirror reflecting the strange unfathomed mind of the colored minority. Expressed in those movements were all its hidden confused reaction, its hopes and fetish fears, its Uncle Tom traditions, its desires, appetites, aspirations, its latent strength and obvious weakness.

10
A NEW SOUL

Buster visited Oleander in Glory Home No. 2. It was the female home and presided over by Glory Queen. Oleander received Buster in the reception room. When he called her Oleander, she said simply, earnestly, that she could not answer to that name for she had been renamed Glory Chastity.

"Don't be telling me that you really believe in that racket," said Buster.

"It's not a racket, it's a true creed," said Oleander. "I joined because I believed."

"Or because you wanted a job?"

"No, I wanted a job, but also I had to believe. Glory Savior is sincere. I'll tell you about him and me. When I joined, I went alone to his office for the holy test. I sat there and he just stared at me like a snake for a long time. And then he went down on his knees and took my skirt in his hands and kissed it. And he said: 'You are pure crystal water. We others, we are old wine with dregs in the bottom. But you, Crystal Water, you must be called 'Glory Chastity.' You see, different people affect him differently. He is our savior. But he is like a doctor who really knows his medicine. He diagnoses the sickness of your body and prescribes the medicine to transform you into a soul. It is possible for him to be all things to all men and women."

"H'm! Are you telling me that you are going to remain that way all your life?" said Buster.

"Oh, you know I was never very physical. So you can understand why this psychic idea was just right for me."

Buster yawned. "I guess there is no hope left for me now," he insinuated.

Oleander laughed: "I can be frank, for I am free. That is what Glory

Savior does to us souls. He makes us really honest to ourselves and to others. I'll tell you the truth. I believe that you were the only person I once felt I could like a lot. But we couldn't do anything about it.''

"You said it," said Buster, "we were both too beat for romance. You know the saying, 'A broke man is a dead man.' And now you're a glorious soul, I guess you never think of romance any more, eh?''

"You know I was never overly physical," said Oleander. "And now I have renounced the physical for the psychic way. I'm happier.''

She stirred up a tumult, perhaps because she was obviously so chaste. He had felt that in her while he was living at Charlotte's. And he had left her alone. She was always apart and aloof from everybody. He knew that she was troubled. And he had too many troubles himself to share anybody else's.

Now in the role of Glory Chastity, she was appealing, fascinating. Like shining copper her features gleamed desire, while she remained indifferent to the fact that she stirred him up so sensuously. She was like a rich ripe tropical fruit, a star-apple on the bough that the birds and the winds had missed and which would not fall.

"You may feel psychic to you and the world, but you are a physical temptation to me," said Buster.

Oleander laughed: "I and everything would be different to you if you were a glory soul. Why don't you join us?''

"Quit your kidding," said Buster.

"I mean it, I do. We have many members like you who have come to us from the theaters and cabarets and they are our best. Our Savior accepts all types of people and finds a place for them.''

"Buster a Glory Soul? Well, I guess this boy has done many stranger things than that in his lifetime," he said.

Just then the Glory Queen entered the room and Oleander introduced Buster. "He is an old friend and I'm trying to get him to join us," she said. "He used to be in the amusement business and is a dancing instructor and music lover.''

The imperious high-breasted Glory Queen appraised Buster and said: "Sure we could use the young man nicely. A dancer and music lover? Why dancing and music is our daily bread.''

Buster sized up Glory Queen and thought: "She could be had. Well, why not be a Glory Souler for a change? Religion is the biggest racket in Harlem. And since we have regular radio music and the slump in the cabarets many of our singers and actors have joined the churches and the cults.''

Buster joined the Glory Souls and was made maestro of music and dancing. It was a great day when Buster became Glory Pilgrim Progress, which was the name that Glory Savior bestowed on him. The ceremonial was held on a Sunday. Glory Savior marched his hosts of souls along Lenox Avenue and Seventh Avenue to the main Glory Home No. 1. There were glory cars with banners and pennants streaming, glory floats carrying white-clad glory boys and girls. Glory Savior and Glory Queen rode together in a magnificent deluxe car.

Although sex was taboo among Glory Souls, Glory Savior reverently respected the outward forms upon which good society was maintained. Glory Savior had selected Glory Queen to fill the place of that carnal lady who had deserted him for Omar, The African.

The main Glory Home was located in a building which was formerly one of the largest synagogues in Harlem. Hundreds were packed into the spacious hall. The walls were decorated with banners and pennants bearing extravagant glory signs. *"Glory to Our Savior!"* *"Glory to the Life!"* *"Glory Eternal!"* *"Glory Savior Sways the World!"* *"All Honor to Our Glory Savior!"* *"We Are All-Souls of Our Savior!"*

Fixed in the rear of the platform was a statue of Glory Savior. Before it was placed two red thrones for Glory Savior and Glory Queen. On either side of them was a row of chairs for the leading souls. In the forefront was a white altar surmounted by a golden cross. The Glory Band was right down in front before the platform. The choir was ranged on either side of the band.

A side door opened leading to the platform and a splendidly tall, green-uniformed brown man stepped up on the platform carrying a large yellow ball, designated as the Glory Globe. Behind him came six little light-brown and dark-brown girls dressed in blue-and-white frocks and bearing candles. They were followed by Glory Queen wearing a blue robe with silver train held up by two pages. She strode haughtily to her seat, her complexion pale like a new window shade.

Another green-uniformed man, heavy, dark-skinned, strode on to the platform bearing an ebony baton. He was followed by six colored boys of varying complexions bearing burning candles. Behind them paced the hefty yellow savior wearing a regal purple suit. "Glory, Glory, Glory!" the people shouted. As the Savior sat on his throne, the attendant upraised the black baton and the band started the Glory Hymn. It was a lilting little tune, designed to tickle the feet and sway the body.

> *My savior he needs me,*
> *My savior he leads me,*

My savior he feeds me,
With glory and glory.

My savior besides me,
My savior he guides me,
My savior provides me,
With glory and glory.

Oh soulfully living,
All love to be giving
And sweetly receiving
My savior in glory.

Again the baton was upraised and at the sign of that smooth piece of ebony, every voice was quiet and every motion was stilled. Glory Savior strode to the altar. With hand uplifted he spoke in a cutting sharp commanding voice. It was not a deep musical persuasive voice like Omar's. It was a voice popping like fireworks, but it possessed power.

"Glory all souls!" he cried. "Glory Savior!" the people responded. "This is another great glory day," he continued. "Another human has transfigurated his life to become a member of our community of souls. He has left the tip-toppers of Harlem, that gin-guzzling, card-playing, numbers-gaming, skirt-chasing, sex-salted gang of fast men and women living in the hide of the body to become a soul. He has left the high places of Harlem, which are like the cloisters of hell where they pound the fire-spurting pianos to make music and dancing for the devil, to seek fellowship with souls because he was overpowered by my glory. My glory struck like lightning and he could not resist. For I am consuming power and benevolent glory. From my unlimited illimitable illuminated high source of sublimity I shed my glory upon humanity to conceive the conception of the divinity of the souls. I am no respecter of classes and creeds and colors and races. My glory is all-penetrating.

"I go down to the lowest in Harlem and I go up to the highest in Harlem for I bring a message with my mission which is maximum and millennium. Harlem must cease from blackness of the body which is consciousness coeval of the indulgence of the flesh to become the reformator of transformation into the national capital of Glory Homes. That is the combination of the culmination of my plan for Harlem.

"Harlem is a sex-pool. We must clean it out with ample sample and example of wholeful and soulful living. That is the seeming and the meaning, the mission and the permission of Glory Souls. Harlem, I say, is a sex-pool, a deep black hole of sweet sin. But I, Glory Savior, discovered and uncovered purity in Harlem when I found Glory Chastity and brought her into the community of souls.

"And today Glory Chastity has rewarded us in bringing us a new soul from the upper realms of biggity and dicty iniquity of Harlem. Glory Chastity recommending and I commending, Glory Pilgrim Progress!"

Oleander, striking in a black-striped yellow dress, walked to the front of the platform with Buster who was in full dress. "Glory Savior," said Oleander and "Glory Savior," said Buster. "Glory souls," said the savior and all the people shouted, "Glory, Glory!"

Standing erect with the upraised baton, Glory Savior signaled the band and Buster whirled off with the Glory jig. Oleander pirouetted around the altar and up to Buster. The Glory Queen majestically capered up and swung between them. Glory Savior leaped to join in nodding his head, his elbows working, his thumb cocked; the candle boys and girls started shivering in unison like leaves agitated by the wind; all the Glory Souls wildly responded to the prompting of the platform with swaying and swinging, singing, shrieking to the highest, transforming the vast pandemonium into a formidable fantastic orgy of shaking feet.

A brown woman fell in the little space before the band, her feet high in the air shouting: "Glory Savior, glory me! Glory Savior, glory me!" A flowing white-haired white man, raising his arms like wings, agitated them over her chanting, "Glory, glory!" Round them whirled the glory dancers, whipped by riotous reeds and thumping tom-tom, stomping out all the pent-up powers of passion. Like a freighted, flooded river overflowing its banks, men and women forbidden by the glory creed to live together joined dancing together. Vivacious youngsters high-kicked like flighty mules, while oldsters found new strength in rheumatic limbs. All the rare ecstasy, the wanton warmth of colored cabarets eclipsed by the Depression and white competition was kindled again in the cults.

11

THE CHALLENGE OF OMAR

JEEHOVAH JITTERS

It's glory in Harlem, the new ballyhooing,
No fighting and killing or drinking and chewing,
No more double-crossing or chiseling and screwing.
Oh, Harlem is hyped with a different behavior,
All Negro no-bodies are souls of the savior,
Exalted to glory by heavenly jitters,
Oh gee, gee, gee, jeehovah jitters!

Oh papa, oh mama, it's you or me next,
Must turn to the savior and follow his text,
Be glory-redeemed from the opposite sex.
Oh, Harlem is hyped with a different behavior,
All Negro no-bodies are souls of the savior,
Exalted to glory by heavenly jitters,
Oh gee, gee, gee, jeehovah jitters!

This rhyme was a variation of one of the Glory Hymns which was sung in the saloons of Lenox Avenue and Seventh Avenue, when Buster's sensational debut among the Glory Soulers became an item of discussion in the black belt. Buster was installed in a good room in one of the Glory Homes for men, but he maintained a small private apartment outside. A car was at his disposal, which he drove himself. He had new stylish clothes and money to spend.

He had won the favor and confidence of Glory Queen, who supervised the expenditures for the female Glory Homes. Often he drove her downtown to make purchases. And frequently Glory Queen visited his private apartment. Although men and women souls resided in separate Glory Homes because of the taboo against sexual relationships, there was unlimited freedom in the cult. All meetings were mixed and male and female souls could visit one another privately in their rooms. But ordinary mortals were forbidden such a privilege.

Also it was a strict regulation, laid down by Glory Savior himself, that none of the acts of the souls within the privacy of the Glory Homes should be revealed to mere mortals. Personal criticism of individual souls by one another was discouraged. All feelings were expressed in open meetings, but in special cases the savior would grant a private hearing. And all the confessions took the form of humility, self-abnegation, self-purging and glorification of the savior.

Nevertheless, there was much whispering, stirring like a snake among the Glory Souls. Buster's flashing among them multiplied the whispering. Buster was a disquieting influence. He was a capable maestro and his dancing was a marvel, but his movements seemed to indicate that he was more preoccupied with body than with soul. Glory Queen's preference for him was remarked and much commented upon.

The rumor reached Oleander. One afternoon Buster took her for a suburban run in his car and she frankly mentioned the matter to him.

"You know they are talking a lot about you and not altogether favorable," she said.

"Niggers will beat up their gums, for all they can do is talk," said Buster, "while the white folks take action."

"Yes, but we who know better must do all we can to protect Glory Savior and our Homes. You are loyal, aren't you?" asked Oleander.

"H'm, yes. But maybe I feel more loyal to you than anybody else among the Glory Souls. You gave me my break."

"You don't have to be loyal to me, but you should be loyal like everybody else to Glory Savior."

"Well, am I not loyal enough? I go to all the Glory Homes everywhere he wants me to lead the dancing and all the Glory Souls look as if they like the way I swing them into rhythm."

Oleander laughed: "Yes, they all like you, but also they all talk a lot about you and Glory Queen going so much together. I wouldn't like that to get to the ears of Glory Savior. After all he is the head and we should all try to hold him and anybody close to him 'way up there."

"I understand," said Buster, "and I'll tell you the truth that I am not doing anything to make people suspicious. Glory Queen likes me to drive her around and I don't mind being her chauffeur. I can't help her liking me any more than the rest of the Glory Souls liking my dancing. But I've never done anything to bring Glory Savior down."

"Honest?"

"Honest," Buster repeated after Oleander, with no compunction about being dishonest. He was too much a man of the world to reveal anything of his relationship with Glory Queen. Was he not trained in the school of Millinda Rose? Moreover, Oleander, alluringly radiant as Glory Chastity, was always exciting his mind, sensually moving and stirring all his amorous instincts. Mingled with this feeling of desire for Oleander was the real respect he felt for her. He had never felt that way about the women of the fast set, who had all taken him as a clever jester to amuse them in any way. He was compelled to take Oleander differently. Upon her suggestion he had joined the cult as a joke, and the whole movement headed by Glory Savior and Glory Queen was a grand joke to him. Only Oleander gave significance to it with her serious faithfulness. Under her sweet influence he had accepted the idea of his job as important technically, while inwardly he mocked at the cult.

"I myself am not accusing you of anything," said Oleander. "I'm only warning you that the souls are talking. Don't let them talk too much, whatever you do. Remember they are colored souls."

"Nigger souls, you mean," said Buster. "Now listen, Oleander—"

"But you must learn to use my soul name, Glory Chastity. Sometimes I wonder if you ever remember that your new name is Pilgrim Progress?"

"Yes, I remember when I am with you. You only make me feel sometimes that the Glory game is a little different from the Numbers game."

"Then, I can count on your loyalty to Glory Savior," said Oleander.

"Yes, I'll be loyal for your sake and also my sake. I'll be a good performer, for I love you, Oleander." Impulsively he kissed her, powerfully pressing her breast against him.

"O-o-o-o-h!" she said, disengaging herself, "that a wrong one."

"No, it's right," he hissed. "That's a real glory kiss."

Suddenly he grew hot and groggy with desire and said, "I'm going."

From Harlem bar to bar, black ones, white ones, Buster boozed through the evening with casual acquaintances, drinking down his high desire. Then he grew weary of whisky-warm faces patterned like a fresco around the bars and took the street alone.

On a Lenox Avenue corner he came upon a huge crowd, dominated by Omar, The African. Black Omar, powerfully tall and stout, was arrayed in Russian boots and American spurs, a Chinese blue cape with Moroccan red lining, an English officer's belt, with his head crowned by an Arabian white turban. Buster stopped to listen, for Omar was denouncing the Glory Soulers.

"Glory Savior is a danger and a disgrace to Harlem and colored America. I say Glory Savior is worse than the lynchers, those crackers in Dixie who would castrate the Negro race. Glory Savior is preaching no-sex in Harlem. I wonder who is paying him to dismember the colored people. He makes the first page of the white man's newspapers, because they like that stuff. Columns and columns of publicity for Glory Savior and none for me trying to organize black labor. Why, Glory Savior is sweet, my colored friends. No sex, no colored babies, no Negro problem. What then? Race suicide? My friends, do we all want to commit race suicide?"

"Hell, no!" the crowd roared.

"Then what is Harlem going to do about Glory Savior? I'll show you a few examples of what it costs Harlem to maintain Glory Homes. Right here on Lenox Avenue Javan Brown rented an apartment for 27 dollars a month. It was a small apartment and Mrs. Brown kept it neat and comfortable. Javan Brown was employed in an importing firm 'way down town. It was a large firm and employed 15 colored porters. Javan Brown was captain of the porters. The firm went down under the Depression and the colored porters had to find them other jobs, or go on relief. Brother Javan was lucky to strike a seaman's job—the same like I used to work at. But the new job took Javan Brown away from home sometimes for months. That was the first time he ever was separated from his wife for such a long spell.

"Then one trip he stayed away longer than ever, for his ship was held up in a strike. And when he finally got back to New York he found his wife acting strangely and saying that she had seen the Savior. He begged her to keep away from that crazy man. But she said that he was no ordinary man, he was everybody's Savior. Brother Brown did not think the thing was serious. He accompanied his wife to one of Glory Savior's meetings. And that was enough, he forbade her to go to another one. His wife said that she would sooner miss sleeping in her bed than a Glory Savior's meeting. Brother Javan laughed and went to sea again. But when he returned he found his wife had left his apartment to go and live in a Glory Home.

"Javan Brown became paralyzed in his actions, and he couldn't go to sea again. I saw him myself in the little dingy room he had rented and kinda loony and all the time gazing at a rag of a chemise belonging to his wife and which he had nailed up on the wall like crucifix. Ain't that a shame, my friends?''

"Shame! Shame!" cried the crowd. "A goddam shame!"

"And there's more yet," shouted Omar. "There's another case you can see right here in flesh and blood. Come on son, stand up and don't be afraid."

The crowd around the ladder opened out to make room for a brown boy of thirteen, who was hoisted up on a barrel in front of the stepladder. The crowd was excited, tense, like soldiers waiting for the signal to go into action.

Cried Omar: "This little boy is an orphan, although his mother is not legally dead. But he became an orphan when his mother announced that she was dead in the body and became a Glory Soul. This boy's father died when he was five years old. And his mother managed to get along working as a domestic and sending him to school. He started selling papers to help himself when he was seven years old.

"He was attending junior high school when, suddenly, his mother announced that she was pregnant with glory and had to go to the Savior. She tried to get the kid to go along with her. (You all know that there also are Children's Glory Homes). But the kid had sense enough to refuse. So she left him alone and went to the Glory Home. And he had to quit school to scram around any way he could for a living.

"Who knows what this boy might have done for his people some day, if he was given the chance to get a real education? Look at his intelligent face! Look carefully, my friends. That face is a man's face, a real man's face in a boy's body. He was man enough not to follow his mother. He was stronger than many of our shot-aced men in Harlem who got beat and turned to glory. This boy is only one example. There are many more like him in Harlem."

The crowd groaned and booed and hissed and cried: "Shame! A shame! Harlem is a shame and a disgrace."

"That is the work of the Glory Savior," shouted Omar. "Colored folks are collected in Glory Homes like the Communists in Russia. But consider the cost, my friends! How many private homes are broken up to make possible Glory Homes? Have you ever figured out that the price that Harlem is paying for Glory Homes? How many of our women have left their husbands and children! Broken homes, broken lives! Do you all know how much money saved in the banks has been withdrawn to be put in Glory Homes? I tell you, you people of Harlem, that it is high time to call a halt. Stop! Listen! Think!

"If we black folk must have religion, I bring you a new religion. I bring you Islam. It is the only religion of true brotherhood and fellowship. And that's what colored folks are turning to glory to find. Islam knows no race and no color. If we must have glory let us build a new church. Let the Savior take his glory to the devil in hell. Throw the Glory Savior out of Harlem and out of the homes of all colored folk. What we need is a work savior."

"You're right, not Glory but work," responded a voice.

Buster was fascinated by Omar's harangue. All that Omar said about Glory Soul was true, he knew. He felt the same things but could not express them, and would never muster the courage to do so, for he himself was a Glory Soul, a holy racketeer. Circulating among the crowd he noticed some young men in uniform and wearing fezzes. He was trying to figure out what was their function, when one of them approached and said, "Hello, Buster!"

"Opal! Why, I would never know you in this grand uniform. What's the racket?"

"Well, it's not a racket," said Opal, "I'm the commander of Omar's Yeomen." There were epaulets on his shoulder-straps.

"Any money in it?" Buster asked.

"Not much, but I believe in it, for it's a part of the labor movement. You remember when we left Newfields I said I was going to join the labor movement. And you, what are you doing?"

"I guess I am your enemy," said Buster.

"My enemy! How come?"

"Well, I was just listening to your Omar talking against the Glory Soulers and it happens that I'm swinging with them."

"Good God, you're with that god-damn gang of holy racketeers?"

"I got a good job swinging among them," said Buster. "The best thing I have struck since I came home from Europe. I tell you, it's the grandest payingest racket in Harlem. And brother, I got to live and I can't live on relief. I got to live as I have always lived. I tried to live otherwise, but I know I can't get away from it."

"Anyway, we can't be enemies," said Opal, "even if we happen now to be going in two different ways. Once a pal always a pal."

"Let's shake on that," said Buster.

The meeting was ended and Opal invited Buster to visit his home. "It's just up the block," he said, "come up and meet the ole lady."

"The same one?" asked Buster.

"Yes, the same ole spade, always digging and dishing dirt, but she's solid and reliable."

"That's the best recommendation. There are so few who are dependable. I got to know pretty early that sex is just a business partnership between male and female in which the man is a one-way street and the woman is a two-way street."

"Perhaps and perhaps not," said Opal, "it all depends on the man. But what about you, pal? Are you off the stuff, now you are a Glory Soul?"

"H'm, we're not allowed to talk to mortals about Glorious affairs," said Buster.

Opal laughed: "You don't have to tell me nothing, pal, you sure look like you are living a glorified life."

Opal was a stocky West Indian brown man, who came to the United States when he was a lad on a banana boat. He had been a member of the Universal-Negro-Back-To-Africa movement. When that movement failed, he drifted unattached to any organization. His wife Mimma was a brown-skinned woman from Virginia, who was generally employed in domestic work.

Mimma was a female Elk. She was not interested in social movements and did not approve of Opal's position as Commander of Omar's Yeomen. She kept nagging at Opal to get a regular job.

Omar's Yeomen of Labor was not a prosperous organization. It had only a few dues-paying members and had to solicit contributions. Its officials and organizers were not regularly paid.

A lady Elk was visiting Mimma, when Opal entered with Buster. Mimma was a shapely woman of forty. Her friend was a bulky brown woman, slightly younger. Opal introduced Buster as his friend from Newfields. Mimma smirked and said: "You might have let me know you were bringing a *gentleman* visitor." She excused herself and disappeared behind the curtained French doors. In a little while she emerged with her hair brushed into shape and wearing a dark green frock.

Opal had opened the pint bottle of whisky he brought in and set four glasses on the table: "Here's to my best pal," he said. "Mimma, Buster knows all the big shots, he is one of them himself, but he is my pal and a damn good one. Here's to Buster and the rest of us—"

"But wait a minute," said Mimma. "You know my stomach can't take that store stuff. I can't drink anything but hooch, Mr. South, excuse me."

Mimma dived down behind her chair and brought up a half-filled bottle of bootleg of the kind that is sold in Harlem for 25 cents a pint bottle. "Here's to you, Mr. South." She poured herself a goodly portion in a large glass and gulped it down, making a face.

"Mr. South," said Mimma, "when my husband told me about meeting you at first, I was kind of skeptical, although he is too radical to make a joke, much less tell a lie. You know I used to read a lot about you and Millinda Rose and the dicty crowd in the *Harlem Nugget*. I'm sore at Opal bringing you here without warning, for I'd have liked to entertain you in style."

"Never mind about doing it in style," said Buster. "I just come up here with Opal like a good old friend."

"Katie," Mimma sharply called to her companion, "can't you sit up like a lady in the presence of a guest?" Large and heavy, Katie, loosened up under the influence of hooch, was sprawling in her chair, her legs wide apart. She straightened herself up just a little to pour a drink from the store bottle of whisky.

"You shouldn't mix yuh drinks like that," said Mimma, "but you're excused to go rest yourself in the next room."

Katie straightened right up and said: "Woman, will you leave me alone? Excuse, indeed!" And turning to Buster in a mincing manner, she said: "Mr. South, I do believe that you know Mr. Hatcher."

"Baldwin Hatcher? Yes, but how did you know that I knew him?"

"How *did* I?" Katie archly eyed Mimma. "Why, I used to work for Mrs. Hatcher and, of course, I overheard them talking about Millinda Rose and you and all the other classy folks in Harlem. The Hatchers, them were nice people to work for."

"They're all right," said Buster, "nothing fake about them. Two pieces of genuine gold."

"Different from the God-forsaken gang of high-society niggers," said Katie, bitterly. "One evening, Mrs. Hatcher she gived a party for one o' them kind. Perhaps you know him, George Sapper. He's a big shot in that there Negro Intelligence Test Society. And Lawd, Lawdy, if I didn't work like a sore-back nigger to put that pahty over from the kitchen. I says to mahse'f: Heah's a nigger gitting honored by high class white folks, there must be some class to him and I felt proud to be a nigger because of that. And I put more of my style in fixing mah stuff than I ever did for any pahty. I put my apron and cap in a special laundry for it. And when I was serving Mr. Hatcher he introduced me to Mr. Sapper in a friendly way like he always introduce me to all his white guests and said I was a jewel and Mr. Sapper should know me. And that colored man he ups and said that he didn't socialize with servants in Harlem. Can you imagine, just like that?"

Buster laughed. "I don't need to imagine, for I know George Sapper is just like that. Why did you quit working for them?"

"Oh, Mr. Hatcher lost his job not so long after I started working for him and gave up housekeeping. I was very sorry but then some of the biggest shots were losing jobs. But they did have the nicest company I evah seen. You remember that Mr. Whippet who write the book called *Interviews*? He made me a present of one with his name wrote in it."

"Oh, yes, Mr. Whippet was a nice person to know," said Mimma.

"And what do you know about him?" said Katie, "except that one day I sent you there to do the scrubbing in place of Joanna."

Opal laughed aloud and Mimma said: "You wouldn't make such a face laughing if you knew how you looked like a damned monkey." She poured the glass full of hooch and gulped it down, holding her throat as if it were hurt.

"Don't drink so much of that rot-gut, Mimma," Opal said, "you'll soon start acting crazy."

Mimma shrieked: "I'll be crazy as madder and crazy can be. You Weshtinjans are so cricketal. You imagine you know all the answers, and you think you are better than the rest of us, but I nevah seen any colored people more *African* than you all. I don't know how come I got mahself hooked by one."

"We don't need a divorce to get rid of each other," said Opal.

"Why, you insulting big stiff! Telling everybody that we're not married, eh? I know your kind is no damned good. I shoulda listened to my sistah when you were running after me all hot and high and she warned me not to fall for a monkey for their tails is too long. I won't stand it no longer," she shrieked, choking and coughing. "I ain't no slow train with the passengers coming and going and not paying the fare, easy riding and getting off at every station. Every woman knows she's no more than an accommodation to a man."

Minna reached for the rest of the hooch on the tray, but Opal grabbed it away from her hand. "Give it to me!" she cried. "It's my money paid for it and not yourn. Gimme, I want another drink." She got up and lunged at Opal, swayed and dropped back in her chair.

"What I wants is eats," Katie yawned, "I feel like a hundred hawgs. Mimma ain't you got no food around?"

That aroused Mimma again who jumped wildly to her feet. "You all come here all the time to drink up my booze and eat my food. I won't stand it no longer, you understand? Get out, all o' you, I didn't send out invitation for no company. Get out, I say!"

She tipped the tray over and began jumping and stamping her feet and screaming: "Get out!" Katie backed into a room and slammed the door and Opal and Buster quickly made their exit.

"That hooch is a knock-out," said Opal. "I believe it's responsible for most of the crazy-acting people in Harlem."

"And marijuana too," said Buster.

"Yes, hooch and marijuana."

"But you would think those people who can afford it would prefer to buy the good stuff," said Buster, "just as a man prefers 15 cents cigarettes to the 10 cents brand."

"It's different with booze,"said Opal, "there's a lot of liquor-heads don't care what they drink, whilst it's strong. And there are others like Mimma, who just love the taste of the bad stuff. I can't get her to drink good liquor, for she likes that raw hooch taste, because she likes to feel crazy like tonight."

"She was rough-house, all right," said Buster.

"Yet I like her a lot, I do. When she gets high she cusses me out for being West Indian, but she doesn't mean anything she says. And I like my American women, believe me. West Indian women are too stiff and backward."

"I like them all," said Buster laughing, "I am international."

"I will walk you over to Seventh Avenue," said Opal. They were still standing on the sidewalk before the tenement.

As they were moving off, Mimma thrust her head out the window and said: "Don't stay away all night now, sugar."

Opal said: "No, I'll soon come back."

"And bring me up some chocolate ice cream," she said.

"Okay."

Buster said: "Oh man, no matter what happens to the world, Harlem is still the same Harlem."

"You're wrong," said Opal. "Maybe you need glasses to see, but Harlem is changing right under your nose."

"I can't see no change in these niggers, pal."

"The Depression made a lot of changes."

"It put a damper on the niggers' spirits, that's all, but they aren't changed, just as shiftless and crazy as ever."

"Omar is doing a lot to change Harlem," said Opal. "It won't be the same Harlem when he gets through with it. In fact it'll be a new America for colored people."

"Listen Opal, do you really believe he can do all he says, more than the big educated Negroes, with influential white people behind them? What has Omar done, so far?"

"Why, he has put colored clerks in the white stores in Harlem. You never saw a single colored man or girl in any of these stores before you went to Paris, did you?"

"That's correct," said Buster.

"Omar said to the white merchants, 'If you exploit the colored community, you must give our people decent jobs. You must give us more than the porter and maid jobs that colored people can get downtown. Now these big, better-class Negroes you mention, they said that Omar was crazy, that if Negroes want employment in stores like white clerks they should open their own stores! And the merchants ignored Omar until he started to picket. They thought the colored public was so dumb and unthinking about labor problems that they would just ignore Omar and flock into the stores like sheep. But when Omar started picketing everyday and talking every night from the stepladder, the colored customers soon got educated to what it was all about. Business got bad in the stores we picketed and soon colored clerks were getting jobs.

"But we are not satisfied with the little gains. We got a long way to go yet. We mean to put over a big thing."

"And can I ask what is that?" said Buster.

"I'll tell you. We're going to picket the big stores in One Hundred and Twenty-fifth Street. That's where Harlem does its biggest shopping, and we want the merchants down there to give our people a break in jobs."

"Fine! And listen, Opal, I am with you. I was with you in Newfields, where I had my first real lesson in labor organization, and I am with you now. I can't join up with you. I'm swinging with the Glory Soulers, because it is an easy racket, but between you and me, Glory Soul is a big swindler. If I can ever be of any use to you, just let me know."

"Let's shake on that," said Opal. They shook hands.

12
HARLEM PICKETS

Buster, elegant in a light brown ulster and driving his burnished chocolate-red coupe through One Hundred and Twenty-fifth Street was arrested in the middle of the block by an animated crowd of people, predominantly colored. It was between Seventh and Eighth Avenues. Policemen on foot and mounted were keeping the sidewalk clear and the crowd overflowed into the street.

Men and women were marching, carrying signs before a large store. Buster saw some of Omar's yeomen and remembered that Opal had told him about picketing in One Hundred and Twenty-fifth Street. It was mass picketing. The signs read:

THIS STORE UNFAIR TO THE COLORED COMMUNITY!
REFUSES TO EMPLOY COLORED CLERKS!

WE DEMAND JOBS FOR THE PEOPLE OF HARLEM!

HARLEM MERCHANTS UNFAIR TO COLORED WORKERS!

BUY WHERE YOU CAN WORK!

WE DEMAND A NEW DEAL FOR HARLEM!

SUPPORT THE YEOMEN OF LABOR!

Opal headed the pickets and gave the cue for the shouting of such slogans as: *"Harlem wants colored clerks!"* and *"We want a new Harlem under the New Deal!"* The comments from the crowd of onlookers showed an interesting mixture of the serious and the lighter side of Harlem. "That Omar may look like a clown in that uniform, but he's got guts," a woman said. "Sure," said her companion, "our colored girls look as good as them white ones waiting on us and never with too much politeness, if you ask me, but white folks don't imagine that colored women are good for anything, besides scrubbing their kitchens and walking the streets.''

"Niggers are waking up," a youth said to his girl. "It is time, we have been sleeping too long," she replied. But an old man remarked: "Negroes can't compel white folks to hire colored clerks: they should open their own stores." "Oh shut up, you!" said a broad woman, "if we spend all our money with the white folks, they ought to give our children a break.''

Harlem was emotionally stirred by its own folks picketing a unit of one of the most powerful groups of chain stores in the United States. When Omar announced his intention of picketing in One Hundred and Twenty-fifth Street, he was laughed at by many prominent and influential colored citizens. The common folk had wondered if he would dare. He had succeeded in getting a few colored clerks employed in the small grocery stores above One Hundred and Twenty-fifth Street which catered exclusively to colored customers. But conditions were different in One Hundred and Twenty-fifth Street, where a considerable percentage of shoppers were white.

Before starting picketing, Omar had sent delegates of Yeomen to interview the management of the stores and demand places for some of Harlem's youth. Every store refused to entertain the idea of employing colored clerks. Some of the managers were rude to the delegates, who were not representatives of the refined colored elements. The owner of one store said that he was a member of the board of a colored charity organization and contributed a sum of money each year. He employed ten Harlemites—four porters, four scrub-women and two female attendants for the ladies' lavatory—but strongly felt that it would be unwise to hire colored clerks. A manager of one of the large chain stores said to the Yeomen: "I am a Southerner and in my part of the country, we keep your people in their place. As long as I am manager of this store it will employ no nigger clerks.''

When the Yeoman reported what that manager said, Omar said: "We will make that store employ colored clerks or get out of One Hundred and Twenty-fifth Street.''

It was remarkable that, in spite of his foreign name and uniform and his advocacy and practice of a strange religion, such a large body of the masses of Harlem followed Omar. But Omar was not so fantastic to anyone who was familiar with the curious composition of the population of Harlem. There were Arabs in Harlem who were more African of the so-called Negro type than hundreds of native Harlemites. One of these Arabs named Abdul was a very devoted follower of Omar, and even conducted classes in Arabic for disciples. Also an interesting number of colored persons who had visited Moslem lands, perhaps as soldiers and sailors, had embraced Islam and legally changed their names after returning to America. There were, besides, semi-secret and occult societies and associations, more or less based upon the Mohammedan creed.

Now when Omar started his movement, the editor of the *Harlem Nugget* published an open statement in which he called upon responsible and authentic Moslems to repudiate and denounce Omar The African as a fakir. But Omar received a blessing instead. An imam from Egypt wrote that no man had any authority to repudiate any person who professed belief in Allah and the prophet Mohammed, for that was the fundamental creed of Islam. It was right after this incident that Abdul the African joined Omar's Yeomen and got other Arabs in Harlem interested in the movement.

But besides the picturesque appearance and harangues, Omar had the sympathy and support of the sane economy-minded Harlemites because he had accomplished something practical for them. It was Omar who pushed colored men into the peddler's business. He organized the first group of men who obtained peddlers' licenses and hired and purchased pushcarts. Harlem laughed, splitting its blacksides, when colored men appeared on its streets selling ice, operating vegetable and fruit stands with peanuts and hot-dogs-on-wheels; even black rag pickers with bells sing-songed to the folks for their cast-off clothes.

Omar said: "You people are ashamed to get out and get low down to do something for yourselves. The Italians and the Jews are not ashamed to bring you your ice and buy your cast-off clothes. You act snooty but they can use that thing to get somewhere, while you remain right there where you won't be able to speak to them when they get up in the world. You are the only colored people I know who are ashamed of exploiting yourself. In Africa the Africans are not ashamed of peddling. The Indians in India and the Chinese in China will put their hands to anything to turn a penny. But you colored folks prefer to get down on your knees on a kneepad behind closed doors in the white folks' home, instead of peddling in the open."

On the evening before the picketing Omar had staged a big meeting in One Hundred and Twenty-fifth Street. At this meeting he justified the line of action he was taking and replied to his enemies and critics, who were numerous in Harlem. Upon his declaring that the colored people needed a new religion, he had earned the enmity of the ministers of the Black Methodists, Episcopalians and Baptists.

Also antagonistic were the colored Socialist and Communist organizers, who unceasingly parroted the slogan: *"Black and White Workers Must Unite!"* and who constantly agitated against the idea of colored workers organizing an independent union.

And also opposed were many influential publicists and apologists of the Negro's status who branded as segregation every effort of the colored minority exclusively to organize and achieve something for the betterment of the group. Such persons even hated the idea of a colored group and opposed the very fact of its obvious existence, holding that the colored minority should do nothing by way of organized effort to accentuate its special traits, but rather should strive towards merging and disappearing among the white majority. They had the support of an important group of whites, liberals and radicals, who, frightened by the racist theories of Nazi Germany, were swinging to the other extreme of denying the existence of biological and geographical sub-divisions of the human species, even to maintaining that there was no such thing as race.

Mounted upon his stepladder, Omar sounded the call to the struggle in One Hundred and Twenty-fifth Street: "The Negro radicals declare that black workers must unite with white and that is the only way. Let the radicals keep on singing the black-and-white blues of unity, but I say there are other ways to go. I say that black people cannot be forever waiting and singing for unity with white people. Hundreds of years before Christianity, the Bible said: 'Ethiopia will stretch forth hands to God.' And, oh God, we're still stretching, begging and singing the same old Ethiopian blues. Twenty unions of skilled workers in the American Federation of Labor declare that black men cannot join, and the Federation can't do anything about it. Now what must our black carpenters and bricklayers and plumbers and painters and electricians and all our other skilled workers do? Always bootleg labor? I say we must organize ourselves and stop whining and begging. Here in America there are Catholic Unions, Jewish Unions and industrial unions and more independent unions. The Jews and the Catholics organize to protect their rights and we got to organize to protect ourselves. My radical brothers declare that we must work and wait for black and white workers to unite. Keep stretching out our hands begging the white worker to take it? The white worker won't grasp a dead black hand I tell you. But if you got a strongly organized hand with something to offer he will grab it.

"And also the black preachers are right after me. People of Harlem, tell your ministers to leave me alone, for I am doing what they cannot do for you. You go to church to pray and sing and the minister takes a collection. But the church can't be a labor union. The Ethiopian Methodists and Baptists didn't get jobs for your boys and girls in the stores. But I got them jobs so they could give something to the preachers. Now the preachers start denouncing me as anti-Christ. My religion is the new religion of labor. Tell your preachers to mind their own business."

"Tell the preachers to pick on Glory Savior," said a voice in the crowd.

"You said the right thing, brother," said Omar. "Glory Savior is taking the people away from the preachers and they should fight him and not me. I am fighting to make Harlem a better place to live in. To inject a new spirit into my people. We got this problem to face: Can we colored folk adjust ourselves to changes in the white man's world? All of Harlem is on relief, waiting for the white hand-out. But the white people exploiting Harlem are shirking their responsibility to the colored people. They take all the profits to spend in the Bronx and downtown. The white businessman is not in Harlem for his health or for charity. They say: Niggers are good spenders. Yes, that's what they say, plain niggers, among themselves. I send my scouts out to listen to some of our white skinned colored. And they can tell you plenty.

"The colored radicals are so constipated with statistics they can't function to help Harlem. They're always writing another article, attacking me in the newspaper, but I never see them in the street among our people. They take statistics to show that colored workers have their best jobs outside of the community. Now what of that? We still have workers in this community. So what? Well, the radicals say that if we organize and ask for more jobs and better jobs in the colored community that the white people who employ colored in white districts will retaliate and the colored people will lose their jobs. I guess the radicals think that Negro labor is no more than a razor-back hog and that white employers are all cannibals. God helps those who help themselves. The white rulers put us in special communities. They are not such fools as to go back on us if we try to make our communities better. If we can do our part to make the colored communities better, we will be helping all of America.

"The radicals don't like me because they're telling colored people: Defend Soviet Russia. I say to my people: Defend black America. The colored radicals are full of confusion from living black and thinking white. I'd like to take a baseball bat and beat their blacksides. My God, right here in Harlem the masses of our people are working for such low wages that they couldn't pay dues into *any* white union. These are the people I am trying to organize and lift up. And these are the people the radicals are telling: Defend Soviet Russia. It is the same old-time religion the black radicals are preaching, but the little lamb is changed to a bear cub. We Negroes have got something to defend all right. We got to defend our community first. We got to wake up to defend our jobs. And we've got to organize as a people to do it. Organize as colored people for a better life.

"But they say I'm advocating segregation. Our educated Negroes object to everything Negro. I can't see any segregation in black organization. Any way we are segregated and what are we going to do about it? I am not advocating segregation, but black folk cannot run away from themselves. Black folk, where will you run to? The white folks don't want you. They'll use you for this thing or that thing and turn you loose again. There are not enough dicty Negroes with money to go in a class by themselves. So as soon as the high-up Negroes move into a new street the low-down ones move right in on them. And what have you? We got to rise together as a people or stay put. When I fight for the black man in the gutter, I am fighting too for the black man with a deluxe car."

So Omar led his followers into One Hundred and Twenty-fifth Street. And the colored folk had turned out in a goodly body to watch the show, some to sympathize and some to deride.

Seeing Buster in the crowd, Opal called to him: "Come on and carry a sign."

"Like hell I will!" said Buster.

"What's the matter, afraid?"

"No, but I'm exhibitionist enough in the Glory Home. I don't want to be an exhibitionist on the white folks' sidewalk."

"It's the colored folks' sidewalk today. Come on," said Opal, "don't be a coward. Remember, you said you were with us."

"I'll show you I'm no coward," said Buster, and taking a sign from Opal he stepped into the picketline.

Buster attracted the attention of some of the girl pickets, who whispered to one another about him. Also some people in the crowd recognized him. Perhaps it was Buster's presence which prompted a svelte brownskin to do her part with more éclat. She was a high school student, who had been unable to finish her education and her ambition was now to become a salesgirl in a high-class store. She lifted up her voice and loudly said: "Don't patronize this store, it discriminates against colored girls."

Apparently she made an impolite remark to an aged colored matron, who was going into the store. The woman stopped and grabbing the girl screamed: "Leave me alone. I'm a free American citizen and will do as I please."

"But I never touched you," said the girl.

"Yes, you have too," said the woman, her wind pipe agitating like a turkey's gullet, "and you ought to be ashamed talking to your betters that way. You're loud and rude. No nice colored girl would go marching up and down the sidewalk talking and acting the way you do."

"Perhaps you'd like to see me prowling along the street at night like perhaps you used to do," said the girl.

"You calling me an old whore? Police! police!" the woman screamed.

The police were right there, plenty of them. "Officer," said the woman to the one who approached, "I want you to arrest this girl for hurting me."

"I never touched you," the girl said.

"Yes, you did everything to me," said the woman.

At that moment Omar in uniform came up. He had been supervising another picketline near Lenox Avenue. His followers cheered loudly. The police tried to stop the demonstration, the mounted ones riding through the crowd and those on foot telling the people to move on.

But some of the Negroes also sympathized with the woman's point of view. Abdul, wearing the red cap of the Yeomen, had attracted a group around him. They were arguing pro and con of the case, some saying that the girl may have a right to picket, but the woman also had her right to enter the shop to buy.

Said Abdul: "The woman is crazy. She want make plenty trouble for her own people."

A dense-looking gibbon-faced fellow said: "But she is American and won't have her rights trampled upon by foreigners." He evidently thought that Abdul was a West Indian and perhaps unnaturalized. Abdul, who was excitable and talked like most Arabs with vigorous gestures said: "You can't eat citizens' rights. We are all colored and should stick together. But you talk like white man. You big fool!" Abdul raised his hands sharply. It was an innocent gesture, but the gibbon, thinking he meant to attack him, quickly drew a switchblade and ripped Abdul in the abdomen. A woman shrieked and a hubbub arose. Abdul held his belly and stumbled back falling against Buster's car. The gibbon disappeared in the melee.

Buster and Opal rushed up to Abdul and helped him into the car. A policeman also squeezed in, and Buster stepped on the gas, rushed Abdul to the hospital.

The girl who had caused the disturbance was arrested with another picket, a man, for disorderly conduct. Also Omar was arrested for creating a disturbance. Standing in the door the officials of the store had watched the dramatic outcome of the picketing with a smug expression. They had refused to make any concessions to the picketers, even to receive a small delegation of the Yeomen and discuss the issues with them. Now they looked as if they thought their action was justified by the result. Perhaps a cynical colored spectator expressed what they thought, when he commented: "The white man don't have to do nothing about niggers, excep'n' give them enough room to fight among themselves and cut their own throats."

13
GLORY SAVIOR AT HOME

Buster hurried away from the hospital, leaving Omar in charge of dying Abdul. He was scheduled to take part in an afternoon shouting at the main Glory Home and was late. Opal had thanked him: "Brother, I didn't know I was getting you into this mess. I was just kinda teasing you, when I challenged you to picket and prove that you were with us. Poor Abdul, he was a splendid worker, a loyal Yeoman."

"Yes, it's a shame," said Buster. "And now I must go back to glory."

He was later than he thought. The Glory Soulers had finished their hallelujah wrestling by the time he arrived. He curbed his car a few feet down from the building, for there were others ahead of him.

Some of the female souls, who were lingering, gossiping, were leaving the building as he was entering. They greeted him with the salute, now universally called Fascist, saying: "Glory to you, Pilgrim Progress."

"Glory all, Glory souls," responded Buster.

"Oh, Buster, there you are at last!" cried a different voice. And there before him in the entrance were Marie Audace and Lotta Sander.

"We thought perhaps you weren't really here."

"Who told you I was here?" he asked.

"I found that out," said Lotta, "trust me for finding out things."

"Well, it sure is marvelous meeting up with you all again like this," said Buster. He led them back into the hall. There were still a few souls there, some meditating alone, others talking together. They sat down. "And what brought you over?" he asked.

"Lotta was coming and then I made up my mind in a hurry," said Madame Audace. "I felt I ought to know New York. I changed my ideas about America."

"And Prince Fanti and Achine Palma and the rest. Did they come too?"

"No, no," said Madame Audace, "but Achine did marry Fanti. The papers were full of it—a crazy business. But now she is more exclusively chic, just a little too snobbish, I think. And she insists on being called Princess Fanti."

"Oh yep," said Lotta, "and now she has her letterheads and cards engraved with an elephant's tusk and coconuts, you know they represent Fanti's Coat of Arms. And when we were leaving she had ordered them to be carved in her furniture."

"And she styles herself the first Afro-American princess," said Madame Audace, "and she is really princely in her manner as much as any of the stupid continental nobility I know. Oh, I do adore Achine: she is so *purposeful*. What you call in America a go-gettem, I believe."

"Go-*getter*, you mean, Marie," said Lotta laughing, "that was so funny the way you said it,"

"And you, Lotta, you didn't marry Baron Belchite?" asked Buster.

"Like hell—"

"Sh-h-h!" said Buster, "this is the temple of Glory."

"Excuse me," said Lotta, "but Belchite, the idea of *my* marrying a man who has no technique for a woman, but is merely a big craphole."

"'Crapule' you want to say, Lotta," said Madame Audace, "sometimes your French gets as funny as my English. But the 'u' is always difficult for the English tongue."

"Gee, there is so much to talk about, I don't know where to begin," said Buster. "But did you all come to stay or just for a visit?"

"I guess I am back for keeps," said Lotta, "life is so difficult abroad."

"And it's hell here," said Buster.

"Well, I am merely a quota visitor," said Madame Audace. "But Lotta is right in a way. Paris has changed. You don't know your old friends. We are all divided into two tissues of right nerves and left nerves." She laughed uneasily.

"They're divided over here, too, even in Harlem," said Buster. "They're always arguing Left and Right, Fascists and Communists, Triskists and Stillinnites, however you pronounce them, colored folks are agitated about everything in the world but themselves, you hear the same argument at a party as you hear on the street or in the gin mill. Colored folks are agitated about Hitler and Mussolini and everything in the world these days excepting themselves."

"Hitler and Mussolini *are* a danger to colored people everywhere," said Madame Audace and a profoundly strange look was in her face.

Madame Audace was no longer the purely 'free spirit' or bohemian aristocrat that Buster had known in Paris. Since those days she had made a pilgrimage to Soviet Russia. She was one of the many of the intelligentsia class who had been influenced by the conversion to Orthodox Communism of the leading French writer, André Gide, who visited Soviet Russia and became a foremost apologist of the Bolshevik regime. Madame Audace visited Soviet Russia, saw what she was shown and returned to Paris a confirmed ''fellow-traveler'' in the Soviet way of life, seizing every occasion to promote the interest of the Soviet system.

But her former bohemian associates were not inclined to listen to too much praise of Soviet Russia. Many of them were very hostile to the Soviet idea. She found herself uncomfortable among those who had formerly delighted in her wit and extravagant energy and enjoyed her singular parties and welcomed her to theirs. She discovered that the free aristocrats who had no objection to meeting her interesting friends from the colored colony of Paris did object to her propaganda on behalf of the freed muzhik. And then something more happened. Some colored politicos were introduced to Prince Kuako Fanti and induced him to become interested in a pan-African movement. Fanti was not keenly analytic of political issues, but he was a gallant prince and proudly African. So with other African and Aframerican intellectuals in Europe he appended his name to a manifesto denouncing the ruthless European exploitation of Africa and proposing reform measures for the African colonial system. Soon following this incident Fanti received a salvo from the Press, through an article purporting to give details of the bohemian life of Paris, in which he was denounced as a very black adventurer, a crook and gigolo, who had swindled sympathetic white friends, women and men, out of large sums of money. Madame Audace, who had special sympathies for colored people as a disadvantaged group, would not believe all the things that were published and rumored against Prince Fanti. She felt that the affair was a matter of political persecution similar to that which was directed against the Communists. Indeed, since her return from her pilgrimage to Soviet Russia, she had often compared the position of the Communists to that of colored people, much to the annoyance of the exclusive colored set of Paris, composed of authentic African nobility, princes and chérifs, students, sons of chiefs and of palm oil and chocolate merchants; officials and scions of French-West Indian rentiers; Aframerican actors, musicians and tourists, whose horizon was far removed from the frontier of the international muzhik. On the other hand, the cynics and wits of her own caste delighted in telling Madame Audace that her conversion had come too late, that she had missed the Communist train and the Dictatorship of the Kremlin was as alien to the world of the international muzhik as the sophisticated colored colony of Paris. So Madame Audace was wandering in something like a social wilderness.

"Well, did you like the meeting?" asked Buster.

"It was marvelous," said Madame Audace, "such a wonderful exhibition of fresh, primitive vitality—if only it could be used for a great social purpose. Perhaps you could introduce me to that Glory Savior?"

"That is easy," said Buster, "just wait here a minute." Buster was happy for the opportunity to introduce Madame Audace, for he had missed the meeting and thought that Glory Savior or Glory Queen might be displeased.

In a few minutes Buster returned and said the Glory Savior would see them. Buster led them to a side entrance and down a corridor to a private elevator which lifted them to the top floor, which had been remodeled for the Glory Savior's private use. A coppery-faced broad beaming young woman ushered them into the reception room. It was an extensive place, the waxed floor bright with a variety of rugs of many colors. It was furnished with expensive divans, and leather cushions and there were four long white benches against the wall, which were used perhaps for those special occasions when Glory Savior held receptions for visiting souls in his private apartment. The walls were adorned with enlarged pictures of Glory Savior and Glory Queen posing together or with the souls in glorious action.

Glory Savior himself was sitting on a white high-backed chair, which was set before a high Gothic window vividly stained with elfin figures and crescents and stars. Round the savior's chair, set back far enough to impart a sense of demarcation, were ranged six large sumptuous chairs, which were for the use of members of his inner circle. There enthroned was Glory Savior, wearing a natty, marvelously chatoyant mauve suit.

"Glory All, Glory Pilgrim Progress," said Glory Savior, saluting, "what tidings?"

"Good tidings, Glory Savior," said Buster. "Visitors from abroad, who heard of your glory works across the seas and have come a long way to greet you, Madame Marie Audace and Miss Lotta Sander."

"Glory, glory," said the Savior, saluting with outstretched hand, but he did not rise.

Not accustomed to saying "Glory," both women bowed and mumbled inaudible greetings. Glory Savior waved them to seats.

"We were at your wonderful meeting and asked our friend to meet you personally," said Madame Audace.

"I am always personally available to all who believe in me," said Glory Savior. "If you cannot reach me in the flesh, you will reach me in the spirit, by the concentrating of your highest spiritual forces upon my personality. The glory which I bestow in my meetings is the same as my personal glory. But whenever time and circumstance permit me and the augurs are favorable, I am willing to be personally contacted in glory."

Madame Audace gazed intently at the yellow man apparently so perfectly at ease ensconced in glory upon his throne. She was struck and amazed by his poise and *sangfroid.* "Even in France you are known," she said. "Your photographs have appeared in the *revues* of Paris and they have written long articles about you."

"My glory is transcendental and global in its universal manifestation. I have received radiant messages of glory from the remote lands of Asia and Africa. There is glory everywhere that expression is seeking to disembody itself from the delusion of the flesh: the celebration of the triumphal manifestation of the forces of mind over body is the potency of universal spirit."

"I am sincerely interested in all vigorous and vital manifestation." said Madame Audace, "and especially in the movements and progressive aspirations of oppressed and persecuted peoples. I feel a special interest in you as a Negro leader."

"Pardon me, but I am not Negro, I am MAN," said Glory Savior.

"And a superb specimen," said Madame Audace, smiling. "But you are a Negro man, *homme de coleur,* is it not so? If I were a man of color like you, with your physical attributes and glorious demonstrations, I would declare myself to the world. Imagine what it means to the oppressed people of your race and color in America and Africa."

"I have no race and I know no color," said Glory Savior. "If I were sentimental to the differential of the species in the conglomeration of humanity, I would be detrimental to the fundamental of the manifestation of glory. I am truly and unruly non-recognition of race and color and creed in the mystical and celestial glorification of all humanity.

"Race and color and creed and nation is damnation of the eternalization of the immortal. God is one and God is all below and above in the diagonal of the diameter of breath and glory in the all-embracing oneness of the expression of God. From glory to glorification is the mission and intention of humanity and the division of souls into race and color and nation and creed must be swept away before the installation of the sublime new system of humanity."

"I believe that you may be right and divinely guided," said Madame

Audace, "especially in these times when a new philosophy of race and color is threatening to divide up humanity worse than it is and to destroy the basis of international understanding. Perhaps the world may need to turn to the oppressed peoples of color for light and leadership. God bless you in your work."

Impulsively Madame Audace rose and knelt before Glory Savior: "You make me feel humble," she said, "and I want to humble myself before your wisdom, for the universality of your outlook."

"Humility is the understanding illuminating of the way to glory," said Glory Savior.

On the other side of the room, opposite the Savior's chair, about six feet of space was cut off by a red rope attached to shining stanchions. Behind was a high door concealed by heavy red drapery. At a signal from Glory Savior, a page pulled back the drapery and Glory Queen with Oleander came forward.

"These are two helping glory souls!" said Glory Savior.

"Glory, glory!" said Glory Queen and Oleander.

"Glory!" said Buster, while Madame Audace and Lotta bowed.

"Pilgrim Progress, we missed you at the midday meeting," said Glory Queen.

"I was held up arranging to bring you these visitors," Buster glibly excused himself.

The door still remained wide open, revealing the bedroom of Glory Savior. The walls were light blue and in the middle of the room was the famous golden glory bed, which all Harlem spoke about. The price of it was fabulous. All the glory souls had made a special contribution to purchase that gilded bed. Although the Glory Queen could not live in that sumptuous apartment according to the laws of the cult, she was still the spiritual partner and supervised the upkeep.

Glory Savior invited Madame Audace and Miss Sander to other Glory meetings: "You are always welcome," he said, "and whenever my person is disengaged and you desire private contact, you are privileged to be glorified by my presence. And you, Madame Audace, you have known Pilgrim Progress in Paris, when he was running loose in the ways of the world. Well, he came back to New York to seek the way of glory. We are all proud of him. You may call upon him any time you want something in Harlem."

Oleander left the reception room with the guests. Outside, Buster offered to drive the two women home. Lotta was living in Harlem and said she intended to stop by the Y.W.C.A. in One Hundred and Thirty-seventh

Street to look up an old friend that was working there. The building was just around the corner and she preferred to walk there. Madame Audace was residing in a hotel in the theatrical district and she accepted Buster's offer.

"Take a spin with us, Ollie," said Buster, "there is room enough for the three of us to squeeze together."

"I don't know if I can go," said Oleander.

"Yes, you can," said Buster. "Glory Savior won't mind anything I do. Didn't you hear how he recommended me to Madame Audace?" Buster pealed a long stroke of sweet laughter.

Said Madame Audace: "I suppose that it is the glory laughter. It sounds delicious. Do come with us, Oleander, that will be so nice." Madame Audace's curiosity was tantalized by the demure but well-poised and self-contained girl who contrasted so strangely with Lotta Sander and other colored girls she had met in Paris.

"Oleander, I mean Glory Chastity, is Glory Savior's heavenly pet," said Buster.

"And what is she to you?" asked Madame Audace.

"Oh, she's my lucky star. She got me my job and protects me from evil."

Oleander smiled and said: "I think you are really a devil in our Glory Home. When do you intend to become a true soul?"

"When you make me," Buster said cryptically.

"I like your Harlem," said Madame Audace, as they sped down Seventh Avenue. "I think I should like to live up here for a change."

"Why didn't you stay with Lotta when you arrived?" Buster asked.

"Because she thought I would be more comfortable downtown with the whites."

"And aren't you?" said Oleander.

"Fairly. I never thought I could like America, excepting the colored people. But I find you are all the same Americans, very interesting. You all have a kind of easy friendly politeness, which you don't find in Europe."

"There's a difference, though," said Oleander. "You'll find out yourself."

Buster dropped Madame Audace at her modest hotel and did not accept the invitation to come in for a cocktail. "Oleander cannot drink," he said, "and they make cocktails better in Harlem."

He drove back through Central Park.

"She seems nice," said Oleander. "I like how she feels about *us*. Funny about some white people. I notice them in the Glory Home. The whites worship Glory Savior even more than the colored. And they don't gossip like the colored.''

"Perhaps they gossip more among themselves," said Buster.

"In the Glory Home we are all together, white and colored," said Oleander.

"Say, Oleander, I've got hold of an idea."

"Well?''

"Well, I was thinking how interesting Glory Savior and Glory Queen looked together today as a symbol of man and wife, while remaining non-physical, non-sex, nothing between them but being the two leading souls in glory. And I was thinking—''

"What?''

"Supposing you and I were married, then we could be the Glory Prince and Glory Princess, the heirs apparent and next in line to Glory Savior and Glory Queen. Both of them like the two of us more than anybody else in the Glory Homes.''

"What a crazy idea, Buster! You're always thinking evil."

"But I'm not, Ollie dear," Buster pressed his knee against hers, "we've got to be practical. Suppose Glory Savior should meet with an accident or something and he should die—''

"But there is no death for souls in glory!" cried Oleander.

"Quit kidding," said Buster, "you and I know that Glory Sublimation and Glory Heavenly Love, who got smashed in that automobile accident are truly dead and buried deep down in the earth. That stuff is all right for publicity, but between ourselves it's something else.''

"If you are a simple believer like me and accept the psychic interpretation of existence, what you believe is true, so if you believe that a glory soul cannot die, it cannot die.''

"Well, if you are a simple believer and accept the physical or psychical interpretation of existence, won't you believe that I love you heart and soul?'' said Buster. "You can have either my physical heart or my psychical soul, but I love you.''

"All glory souls love one another," said Oleander.

"Can't you be serious?''

"About what?''

"My proposal.''

"If you are really proposing to me, I think you might be more romantic in expressing it, more like a man of the world, who has lived in Paris. But you keep mixing up the physical with the psychic, that's so confusing.''

"That comes from my being a confused glory soul," Buster laughed.

"Well, I'll be precisely romantic. Since there are a Glory Savior and a Glory Queen, in the Glory Home, why can't you and I be the Glory Prince and the Glory Princess, legally." He held her hand tightly and said: "Don't answer me now: think it over."

14
A STRANGE FUNERAL

Yeoman Abdul had died in the Harlem Hospital from his stab wound, and Omar had arranged to give him a Moslem funeral. The Yeomen's Hall of Lenox Avenue was converted into an improvised funeral chapel. The spacious and rather dilapidated old hall was formerly one of the largest and gaudiest Negro saloons and cabarets in pre-Prohibition Harlem.

The funeral was held on a Saturday evening. The body had been on view all day and a stream of humble Harlemites had passed through the building to see it. The casket was set upon a bier right before the platform. The body was tightly swathed in white and Abdul's red fez was set on his head. There were floral contributions sent by individuals and societies. From the ceiling in the forefront of the platform right over the casket, there was suspended a red banner in the middle of which was fixed a huge golden crescent.

Apparently Omar had underestimated the strength of his movement among the people of Harlem, or he would have obtained one of the big casinos for the funeral service. Long before the hour for the service, the hall was packed. Secret and mystical societies, which Omar never imagined might have been touched by his movement, were unexpectedly represented. There were delegations from the Builders of the Pyramids, the Sheiks of Arabia, the Mullahs of Morocco, the Daughters of Medina, all wearing marvelously colorful regalias and turbans or fezzes. Besides the Aframerican proselytes, there was a representative group of Moslems from Egypt, East Africa, West Africa and North Africa; the majority of them, however, wore conservative American clothes. Few Aframericans in Harlem were aware of the large colony of Africans in their midst. Like colored Americans, the Africans were of varying complexion, from ebony to ivory and the so-called typical African of legend and history could be more easily identified among the Aframericans than the Africans of Harlem.

By the time the service began the sidewalks were animated by a crowd vastly greater than that inside the hall. Omar had requested an imam from Egypt to conduct the funeral service. The imam was a brown man who without his robes might have been just like an ordinary American mulatto. In his burnous and turban he seemed very foreign.

"Allah, il la ha, il la la hi, Mohammed Rasul lu, la hi," (God is great and Mohammed is his prophet). For half an hour the imam chanted and prayed in Arabic, continually repeating the refrain, "Allah, il la ha, etc." And the women of Harlem wept and moaned and men murmured, "Amen," although they did not understand the words.

The imam ended in English, clipped, precise, effective. "Many of you not seen before Moslem funeral, nor been in any Moslem meeting. In Moslem land a funeral is a simple thing. No casket, no flowers. We think more of spirit of dead than body. We Moslems worship the spirit of our great and good souls. They are our saints. We keep them inside hearts. So I can only ask you people of Harlem to do for Abdul, what his people in Africa would do. Carry Abdul in your hearts, think well of Abdul, remember Abdul.

"He came a stranger to live among you. He found death here. But also he found life here among you, his lifework. He saw great work for people of Harlem to accomplish. He joined in that work. He followed your great leader, Omar. He was a faithful follower. He died as a soldier among you, for you. Remember Abdul."

The imam called Omar to speak. Omar, long-booted and spurred, in white cap and turban stepped to the front of the platform. Omar began telling how first Abdul joined his Yeomen of Labor in the beginning of its formation. They had accused him in the colored newspapers of being a labor fakir, and racketeering in a strange religion. And Abdul had come to him simply affirming his faith and saying that any man who worked for his people in the spirit and with the name of God must be a good man. Abdul was a martyr for the cause of colored people and the cause must go on as a monument to Abdul.

"Friends and followers, people of Harlem, they accuse me of being a racketeer. But if I wanted to be a big shot racketeer, I would have continued in partnership with Glory Savior. I would have trained you to shout: I'm a Glory Soul with no body, no sex, no problem of race or color. Glory Savior has many mansions, glory homes, glory lands, glory cars, glory boats, glory cattle. I have nothing but this old building, which belongs to the Yeomen. I have nothing but my faith in my people. I have faith that you will turn your back on the old glory stuff and rise up to save yourself as a people.''

A loudspeaker had carried Omar's voice to the street. And as he finished, the audience exploded with applause. The imam stood and stretched out his hands over the casket in an appeal for silence. But the frenzy was prolonged. The contagion carried to the crowd outside and swept the block, the people shouting, ''Omar! Omar!'' So great was the tumult that a frightened soul turned in a police alarm under the impression that the grand emotional demonstration was a riot starting. Police cars clanging dashed to the scene. The cops were ready to swing into action. But Omar, warned of the danger, had hurried outside through a side door. Pushing his way into the thick of the crowd dominating with his size and conspicuous uniform, he thrusted aloft his hand and thundered: ''It's a funeral! Silence! A funeral!'' The police, also subdued, contributed their best effort to relieve the situation and help the traffic, restricting the crowd to the sidewalk and keep it circulating.

It was a people's funeral. The professional strata, the smart fringe of the neighborhood's life, were not represented. But the intelligentsia, by proxy, was perforce represented by the newspapermen. Foremost among them was the editor of *The Nugget*, liveliest of Harlem's weeklies. He was a highly educated person out of a leading New England college, who had increased his culture by postgraduate studies abroad. He considered himself the peer (and was educationally qualified to be) of his white fellows, even though not accepted in their group, and was consequently a little embittered generally and specially skeptical about any movement of the colored masses. He despised Negro journalism and even himself for being identified with it, when his talents entitled him to a superior field. But even his cynicism was momentarily disarmed by the overwhelming emotional demonstration of the people.

So he said to the *Nugget* photographer, who was pleased to have flashed some excellent aspects: ''That was really an impressive crowd. But I can't understand how those people were so patient and serious all the time listening to that imam, though they couldn't understand the language he was speaking. Do you think our common people, dumb as they are, could really work up any enthusiasm for a new religion?''

''They listen to the Catholic priests doing their stuff in Latin, which they don't understand either,'' said the photographer. ''Yet there are many colored Catholics, thousands of them. If you have colored Catholics, why can't we have colored Buddhists or Moslems or what else?''

''Perhaps you're right,'' said the editor.

15
GLORY SHAKE

I t was glory hallelujah evening at Glory Home Number One. All the souls were wallowing in sweet joy of singing praise to the savior:

> *The love of our savior is vast and deep,*
> *He loves and protects us awake and asleep,*
> *He guides us and feeds us, his submissive sheep.*

Buster in evening clothes, neat like a prancing black colt, dominated the glory orchestra under his baton. The music banged crashing into the body of the people, the saxophone running the warm melody like a high wind stirring tall bamboo trees, the drum beating like a galloping horse.

Buster jerked himself, sidestepped and reared, pointed his baton at the savior seated on his throne and then waved it from the orchestra to the people, who, frenziedly, wildly swaying, outstretched their hands as if they desired to touch the baton:

> *He leads me, he leads me,*
> *My savior he leads me.*

The bedlam shocked the hall and gathered crowds in the street. Choosing his moment, Glory Savior leaped with a glorious yell from his throne, started cutting keen capers round the platform, Buster stepped down out of the picture.

"Oh, Glory Savior, Glory Savior!" Men, women and children, white and colored, all dominated by the vigor of the figure on the platform, shouted his name and danced, emulating his steps. Glory Savior regulated the pulse of the crowd, and when the high fervor showed an indication of subsiding, he stretched forth his hand and stopped the dancing.

"Now glory voices will bring praiseful expression of inmost thoughts," he said. A young woman rushed upon the platform, crying, "Glory, glory!"

"Glory to all souls! Glory my savior! Oh, my savior, I was a wrong-way woman. I was too light-skinned among dark men, who came rushing, exploring me like a gold mine. Oh, Glory Savior, I was a deadly woman, and hated by all women, because men found joy in me. I was stepping high and proud, when suddenly I heard your glory calling me. Oh, the thunder did roll and the lightning did flash and I heard the voice of Glory Savior calling me. Calling me and saying, Cleopatra Price, it's your savior call-ing: you been kicking too long against the pricks. You got to turn over a new leaf and go down another street and I will be your guide.

"But oh, my savior, I didn't want to turn over for anybody's new leaf. So instead of turning over I turned against you, fighting glory. And I wrastled with you. But you were strong, my savior, stronger than all the men put together I ever did have. For you slapped me down to the ground, me, Cleopatra, and you stomped upon me and I liked it and cried: Glory. Oh it was good and it was great, glory burning me up. Glory grabbed me and gripped me so hard, I was paralyzed with sweet joy, with glory inside of me filling me up and glory all over me. Glory jazzed me and razzed me, Glory slammed me and jammed me round and round until I was glory crazy.

"Oh savior, you have given me joy and love in life, all that I never had when I was whirling whoring round the world. Now I am no longer consorting with Satan and his angels. I am as white as a dove because of your glory, which you planted in me to grow like a big tree.

"Oh my savior, I was over-sexified, but now I am chastified by your glory. It makes me sweet, it makes me high; it makes me feel happy like up in the sky. It makes me sing, it makes me dance. It makes me laugh and live and love in glory, sweet glory."

As the young woman stopped, Glory Savior leaped to the center of the platform, barking: "It's glory, great glory, I am the glory savior of souls." The cymbals banged and the people sang:

> *It's glory hallelujah, hallelujah, oh glory,*
> *Oh lightning like glory, oh thunder, it rolls,*
> *And it rains, glory raining proclaiming the story,*
> *Hallelujah, my savior, Glory Savior of souls.*

Glory Savior, with skillful daring capers and clapping of hands kept the people to dancing and singing interminably. He felt that no other glory voice that evening could say anything approaching the frankness and in-tensity of the words of Cleopatra Price. And as a shrewd manipulator of holy crowds, he did not desire an anti-climax. Even though he carried on his work in the tradition of the old-time religion, he was no loosely-shuffling old-time preacher, depending on spontaneous inspiration only. He was a first-class impressario. Each glory meeting was like a theater piece or an animal act in a circus. He prepared himself carefully, thinking out new items to enrich the ritual and seizing upon every new manifestation among his large following to increase his power.

As the dancing and singing continued, some of the people crowded on to the low platform, dancing and shouting around Glory Savior. Women and men flung out their arms wildly and kicked, some actually throwing off their shoes and other articles of clothing. Sometimes it seemed as if they were preparing to do a striptease. It seemed that such a frenzied tumultous orgy, expressive of the most primitive emotions, would ultimately explode into a spectacular finale.

But at the precise moment, Glory Savior started singing the "Glory Shake":

> *Let us shake hands and be happy,*
> *Oh shakem, shakem, shake,*
> *Shaking, shaking all together,*
> *Let glory have a break.*

> *All glory souls are happy,*
> *Shake hands, shake hands,*
> *Your savior is commanding,*
> *Shake hands, all lands,*
> *Oh shakem, shakem, shake.*

As he started the singing, Glory Savior began shaking hands with all those around him. And all the people imitated him, shaking hands with one another and dancing and singing and shouting greetings until the scene appeared like a great carnival of friendly feeling.

Meanwhile, Buster, finishing his special job, had slipped away and gone home. He had been up drinking the night before and his strenuous part at the beginning of the performance had tired him out. He went home straight to bed.

But Glory Queen, with her possessive interest in Buster, had remarked his absence. She wondered if he were carrying on another secret affair. She knew that he still kept up all his contacts with the fast world, although he was an active member of the cult. Buster's excellent performance had affected her like a stimulant and the warm collective body of the people pressing upon her had excited her to high desire of more individual contact. And so at the height of the tumult of singing-dancing and shaking hands, she disappeared from the scene and hurried to Buster's apartment.

Buster turned from one side to the other as the pounding on his door disturbed his sleep. His bell was out of order. He pulled the cover over his head, as if he thought that would prevent him hearing. Then, exclaiming, "Oh hell!" he shuffled to the door. As he opened, Glory Queen heaved in, falling upon him.

As always inclined to follow the way of least resistance, he went down under the tempest of passion, which swept Glory Queen into his rooms.

Always wistfully reserved and self-contained all through her experience with the cult, Oleander was also affected by the general contagion. The common flame of the warm movement of the people was also lit in her. She was exalted in a different way, the general handshaking shooting thrill after thrill through her. All her natural reserve was broken down.

Oh, if only Buster was there! Touching *his* hands would have a deeper meaning for her. She would like to feel his hands laid upon her, drawing her away from all the other hands, encircling and holding her close to him. She would like him to know how she felt. She could tell him freely, frankly how she felt. She was urged to go to him.

Oleander eased out of the tumult and made her way to Buster's apartment. She took the self-service elevator to the third floor. There was no answer to her ringing. Observing the door was not locked, she thought she would give Buster a surprise and went in. She tiptoed along the corridor and into the room, where Buster and Glory Queen were together on the couch.

From her position, Glory Queen saw Oleander first and both women screamed at once. Glory Queen rose up to the height of anger crying, "Buster, you common dog! This is a trap, a trap."

Buster in a daze straightened himself upon the couch and tried to explain: "Oleander, please—"

Oleander was crying. Glory Queen turned to him in a rage. "You skunk, you louse, you damnable no-count and dirty thing, you framed me with her—yes, you did. Gahd, I'll beat your brains out, you filthy hawg!" Grabbing her shoe, she brought the heel sharply down upon Buster's skull. Oleander ran out of the room.

"Gee!" he hissed as the thing stung his brain, and grabbed Glory Queen by the wrists, "Stop fooling! Good God, what a jam you've got me in. Oleander will never speak to me again."

"Me got *you* in a jam!" Glory Queen cried. "I am the person in a jam and you planned it, you swine, with that sweet and innocent sister. But whatever you're after, you won't get anymore than you got already. You can't blackmail me or Glory Savior. You understand? You left that door open on purpose—"

"You did it and not I," said Buster, "you were in such a hurry, you almost rushed me off my feet."

"You're a liar and an insulting dog if you say I was in a hurry," said Glory Queen. "In a hurry for what? I guess you imagine you are the hottest thing in Harlem."

"Lawd, I wish I was dead," Buster groaned. "I sweared to Oleander that there was nothing between me and you. Now she'll never have anything to do with me again. And she's the only gal in Harlem."

"Why, you disgusting whoremaster," cried Glory Queen. "So you were really fooling with that slut! And she had the nerve to pose as Glory Chastity, the little hypocrite, I'll beat her black skin blue. And when I get through with her she won't fool again with any man I like. O-o-oh, when I lay these hands on her! Let me get her now."

Glory Queen made for the door, but Buster dashed past her and blocked the way: "Woman, are you crazy?" he said. "Don't you realize you got no clothes on?"

Buster pushed her back to the couch and she calmed down under his hand. She sprawled face downwards on the couch and started crying. "I am ruined, I'm a lost soul. Glory Savior will hear all about this and put me out of the Glory Home. I'll be dethroned and that wench will be put in my place. Oh what a disgrace. Poor Glory Queen! What will become of me now?"

She lay on the couch moaning and shaking a long interval. At last when she faced up she found that Buster had gone. She jumped up wildly, getting into her clothes. "He's left me to go to her. Played another trick on me after all I've gone through for him. Ungrateful, no-count, double-crosser, like all the niggers in Harlem. I'll kill 'em; I'll find them if they're hiding in hell."

[HERE THE MANUSCRIPT ENDS.]